Joy Avery works as a customer service assistant. By night, the North Carolina native travels to imaginary worlds—creating characters whose romantic journeys invariably end happily ever after.

Since she was a young girl growing up in Garner, Joy knew she wanted to write. Stumbling onto romance novels, she discovered her passion for love stories; instantly, she knew these were the type of stories she wanted to pen.

Joy is married with one child. When not writing, she enjoys reading, cake decorating, pretending to expertly play the piano, driving her husband insane and playing with her two dogs.

Also by Joy Avery

In the Market for Love
Soaring on Love

Discover more at millsandboon.co.uk

CAMPAIGN FOR HIS HEART

JOY AVERY

MILLS & BOON

First Published in Great Britain 2018
by Mills & Boon, an imprint of HarperCollins*Publishers*
1 London Bridge Street, London, SE1 9GF

Campaign for His Heart © 2018 Joy Avery

ISBN: 978-0-263-26522-4

0818

MIX
Paper from
responsible sources
FSC™ C007454

This book is produced from independently certified FSC™
paper to ensure responsible forest management.

For more information visit: www.harpercollins.co.uk/green

Printed and bound in Spain
by CPI, Barcelona

Dedicated to the dream.

Acknowledgements

I acknowledge everyone who continuously supports
me along this beautiful journey!
I love and appreciate you all!

Chapter 1

Lauder Tolson sat on the edge of his desk, tossing a stress ball into the air and listening to his best friend and campaign manager, Chuck Carlisle. The man went on and on about the fact that he needed to appear more family oriented if he wanted to win the senate seat, especially in the great state of North Carolina.

Six months until the election and Lauder still couldn't believe he'd actually decided to run for congress. *A bold move, Tolson. A bold move.*

Chuck—or Chuckie, as Lauder liked to call him—snapped his fingers, drawing Lauder's attention back to the conversation.

"You with me? You listening?" Chuck said. "This is serious, L."

Lauder tossed the ball to Chuck. "Think fast."

Chuck knocked the blue puff across the room. "I need you to focus."

Lauder rubbed a hand over his close-shaven head. "Calm down."

"These aren't calm times." Chuck paced. "I know that snake in the grass Edmondson has something up his dingy white sleeve. I can feel it."

Jeff Edmondson had been a thorn in Chuck's side since

the man had decided to throw his hat into the race some months back. If being a family man was what would win the race, Lauder should drop out now, because Edmondson had him beat in that arena. The man had been married for countless years to his high-school sweetheart and had enough well-mannered children to start their own baseball team. But what the man lacked, in Lauder's opinion, was passion. Edmondson wanted the win because *Senator* preceding his name would add to his prestige. Lauder wanted to win because he truly wanted to make a difference in his home state and in a foster care system that had failed so many, including him.

Chuck stopped so abruptly he nearly stumbled over his own feet. "We have to polish up your image, and fast. You need a significant other. Now." Chuck massaged his clean-shaven jaw.

Lauder knew that cunning look on Chuck's face. The man was up to something. Something Lauder was sure he wouldn't like. Lauder's brow furrowed and lips parted, but Chuck cut him off before he could speak by tossing a hand up.

"Before you get all *I don't do long term,* it doesn't have to be a real relationship. It just has to appear that it is. In the political game, it's all about perceptions," Chuck said.

Nope, he didn't like it one bit. Lauder folded his arms across his chest. "Let me get this straight. You want the man running on a platform of truth and accountability to lie about having a lover. And on top of that, you expect me to convince someone to be my fake girlfriend."

"Wife."

Lauder pushed to a full stand. "Wife! Hell, no!"

Chuck massaged the back of his neck. "Okay. Girlfriend will work. Unless you are just totally against a fake wife. That would play so much—"

Lauder shot Chuck a death stare.

"Girlfriend will work." Chuck started to pace again. And stopped again. "But none of the women in your little black book. Those women would do more harm than good."

"I'll have you know I only deal with the cream of the crop."

Chuck released a condescending laugh. "Yeah. I'll handle it. I know your type. I'll make sure I choose the opposite."

For kicks, because no way would he ever entertain such a ridiculous idea, Lauder said, "Shouldn't I have a say in whether or not I want to parade around town with some stranger on my arm for the next several months?"

"*Wayment*. You're telling me you're okay with a stranger in your bed but not on your arm."

It always tickled Lauder when uptown and proper Chuckie allowed his hoodness to slip out. But since they were having a serious conversation, he bit back his amusement. Plus, he had him there. He'd never favored attachments. He was a product of his past. And that past had taught him not to get used to anything or anyone.

"First off, I'm a thirty-six-year-old *grown-ass* man. Whom I allow in my bed is still my damn business. No one else's."

"Lauder…" Chuck paused as if to get his thoughts together. "You're running for a state senate seat. Your business *is* everyone's damn business. Welcome to politics."

Lauder dropped into his chair and massaged his now throbbing temple. What in the hell had he been thinking running for congress? He was a businessman. He wasn't a politician. Why in the hell hadn't he kicked Chuck out of his office when he'd first approached him with the idea?

"You'll make a hell of a senator," he'd said. "You can change the world."

Lauder scoffed, remembering his friend's words. *Change the world.* All he wanted to do was change North Carolina. Tackle homelessness, poverty, foster care. Definitely foster care. A severely damaged system, in his opinion. That alone still made this journey so worthwhile.

"When did this crusade to polish my image become an agenda? My wifeless, kidless image hasn't been a problem before," Lauder said.

"Before Edmondson started parading his trophy wife and his perfect little renditions of himself all around town in their color-coordinated outfits, smiling and waving like they're on a parade float." Chuck grimaced, then started again, "This is the south, L. The perfect family allusion works on multiple levels. You do want to win, right?"

"Yeah, but you want me to lie to get what I want."

"You say it like it's a new concept. Politicians have been lying since the beginning of time."

"But I'm—"

"Not a politician," Chuck said, continuing Lauder's thought.

"Exactly. And that's not how I want to build my campaign. Not on lies."

Chuck rested his hands on his hips, lowered his head and sighed. "What do you want to do, L? You want to drop out of the race? Concede to Edmondson before there's even been an election? Bow down to the same cocky bastard who said you didn't stand a snowball's chance in hell against him?"

Hearing Edmondson's words hurled at him caused his jaw to clench now, just as it had when the self-entitled jerk had first spewed them to a room full of reporters.

Chuck leaned against Lauder's desk and eyed him. "Tell me what you want to do, L? I'll support whatever decision you make."

Lauder stood with urgency. "I want to get a drink." A second later, he ambled to the door.

"You don't drink," Chuck said.

"I'm about to start. That's what politicians do, right?"

Several minutes later, Lauder stood in line inside the Drip Drop Coffee Shop, eyeing the board as if today would be the day he strayed from his usual order—iced cinnamon caramel macchiato. *A creature of habit.*

He slid his gaze from the board and skimmed his surroundings, snatching his eyes back to a table situated in a dimly lit section of the restaurant. *Couldn't be.* His eyes narrowed on the brown-skinned woman beaming at something on her tablet screen.

A flash of light from the device highlighted her features and that scar. The one above her right eye. The one he'd given her so many years ago when he'd been attempting to hit a tree, but had dinged her instead. Every cell in his body fired all at once, sending a longing through him he hadn't felt in years. Close to twenty to be exact, because that was how long it had been since he'd seen her. Willow Dawson. The only woman who'd ever claimed a piece of his heart.

Willow could feel the presence of evil before her eyes rose to face it. Without the man in front of her uttering a single word, she instantly recognized him. Lauder Tolson. Candidate for a North Carolina senate seat and her childhood nemesis.

Something fluttered in her stomach when she inhaled a whiff of his cologne. Ignoring the violation, she gave him a quick perusal, one that revealed a lot of change. This was not the gangly, pimple-faced boy she remembered. This was a full-grown man. Easily six-four and as solid as a brick wall—an extremely sturdy, wide-shouldered brick wall—with dark, daunting eyes that bore into her.

An unexplainable heat circled her neck, rose to her ears and settled in her cheeks.

"Weeping Willow."

His smooth, deep timbre caused her skin to prickle. She prayed he hadn't noticed. When his full lips curled into a lopsided smile, she almost forgot he'd broken her heart when they were younger.

Fighting the urge to show her teeth and growl, she said, "I hated that name then, and I hate it even more now." Not only because it was mocking, especially coming from Lauder, but because it reminded her of a past she wanted to forget.

Lauder rested his hand on the back of the chair directly across from her. "May I?"

"I'd prefer you—" she stopped when Lauder eased down, blatantly ignoring her impending objection "—didn't." She sighed, pushed her tablet aside and leveled an emotionless, hard stare at him.

Her first mistake.

Despite whatever lingering distaste she held for the man, she couldn't deny how good-looking he was. Even more attractive in person than on television, attempting to convince everyone that he was the right candidate to represent them. He'd definitely grown into a fine…very fine man. She wasn't sure which was smoother, the molten chocolate latte she sipped on or Lauder's deep chocolate skin. Neither was good for her, she reminded herself.

No, this was not the man—boy—she remembered.

"It's been a long time," he said, taking a sip from his cup. Willow ignored how his full lips wrapped around the plastic lid. Unscrambling her lust-laden brain, she said, "Some would say not long enough."

Lauder chuckled and smoothed a hand over his stubble. She noticed the absence of a wedding ring. But she already knew he was a bachelor, never married and no kids from the interviews she read online. The Lauder she'd once known had been an asshole. Lauder the politician held her attention. Especially when he talked about the big plans he had for the foster care system in North Carolina.

"Come on, Willow. It's been close to twenty years. Are you still holding a grudge?"

Was he serious? After what he'd done to her? Did he think that even after all of this time she could forgive him? Tamping down the fury rising inside her, she flashed a broad smile. "A grudge? Of course not. How could I possibly resent the man who made my life a living hell?"

Which wasn't all true. At one time, he'd made her happier than she'd ever been in her life. He'd made her feel wanted, which had meant so much to her since she'd grown up in foster care feeling unwanted all of her life. Then he'd shattered her heart.

Lauder's expression turned sad. "People change. I've changed."

"Really? Well, I wouldn't know because you—" She stopped abruptly before revealing too much. What did it matter after all this time anyway? The past was the past, and she preferred to leave it right where it was.

"You should get to know me, Willow. I promise you'll like this new and improved, much more mature version."

Get to know… Ha! Was he serious? He couldn't actually be suggesting they spend time together, could he? Beyond the five minutes she'd already endured? She studied the no-nonsense expression on his face. Yep, he was dead serious. "I'll take your word for it." She collected her things and made a motion to stand.

"You haven't always hated me, Willow. And truth be told, you don't have a reason to hate me now."

In a bold move, he reached over and slid the pad of his thumb across the scar above her right eye. Her forever reminder of him. She snatched away, his touch infuriating her even more than his words had. She did have a reason to hate him. "I allowed my guard down once and trusted you with…" She stopped and cleared her throat when her voice cracked. Refusing to relive the angst of their past, she stood. "I have to go. I would say it was nice running into you, but it wasn't."

With that, she walked away from the man who'd long ago walked away from her and had never looked back. Neither would she.

Chapter 2

For the past week, Lauder hadn't been able to think about anything but Willow. Even now, in the back of the sedan on his way to an interview, he studied the picture of Willow on the About Us page of her company website.

He liked her brown hair cut in that sassy, short style. It gave an unobstructed view of her neck. Man, his lips yearned to explore that neck. She was far more beautiful in person than on a screen. Though he knew it was real, recalling seeing her in the Drip Drop felt like a dream. *A dream come true.*

"I guess there's no changing your mind about her, huh?" Chuck asked, seated in the back of the chauffeured vehicle with Lauder.

Without looking away from the screen, Lauder said, "Nope. She's definitely the one."

Lauder had agreed to Chuck's charade, but with one condition: Willow played the part of his would-be lover. Chuck had rattled off his objections, but in the end, Lauder had made it clear that it was either his way or no way.

Now, all he had to do was convince Willow. And judging by the icy reception he'd received from her, that wouldn't be easy. But he liked a good challenge.

"The one?"

Lauder could hear the surprise in Chuck's tone. This brought Lauder's gaze to him. "You know what I mean. She's the perfect one to play this part. We have history. That'll make this thing appear much more authentic."

"Uh-huh." Chuck rummaged through his briefcase, removed a stack of binder-clipped papers and flipped through them. "History you probably should have thought to mention to me. The fact that you two resided in the same group home for a while does play well."

"It didn't— Wait. How do you know that?" Lauder scrutinized the papers Chuck held. "What are you reading?"

"You didn't think you could send me an email stating you'd found the perfect candidate to play the part of your fake girlfriend and not expect me to vet her, right? And for future reference, it's best we talk about this face-to-face."

Lauder laughed to himself. Chuck sounded as if he was running for the presidency. No one cared what was in his emails. Still, he nodded his agreement, then said, "Vet her? You had Willow investigated?"

"Don't sound so surprised. I have a dossier of people attached to this campaign. Politics can be ruthless. I want to make sure we're not blindsided."

Lauder was unsure how he felt about Chuck invading Willow's privacy or the privacy of the others in his camp. "This feels an awful lot like crossing the line, Chuck."

"Calm down. Most of the information is public knowledge."

"*Most?* And how was the rest gathered?"

Chuck sent a gaze in Lauder's direction, the look on his face suggesting Lauder didn't want to know. Lauder shook his head and slid his attention out the window.

This was the murky part he hated about politics. How far was too far?

Chuck continued to peruse the papers. "Her credit score is better than mine. Highly respected in the law enforcement community. Her company does a lot of work with Raleigh PD. Obviously, she's good with her hands because she's won a ton of awards for her clay work." Chuck flipped several more pages. "Uh-oh."

Lauder whipped his head toward Chuck. "What was that for?" When Chuck didn't readily respond, Lauder leaned in to see for himself.

Chuck moved the pages out of view and laughed. "Chill, man. You're invading my personal space."

"What the hell is *uh-oh*?" Lauder couldn't explain his dire need to know what had happened in Willow's life that would warrant an uh-oh. An urge to wrestle the man for the papers came over Lauder, but he resisted.

"Seems Ms. Willow Dawson has been bitten by the baby bug. She has a pending adoption application. Looks like she tried to adopt once before. A kid she'd been fostering."

"What happened?"

"The application was denied."

Lauder's brow furrowed. "Denied? Why?"

"'We feel the applicant lacks a stable enough home structure and financial outlook to support adoption at this time,'" Chuck read. "It looks like she was just starting her forensic facial reconstruction company and had quite a bit of her finances tied up in it. The social worker made a note about not believing Willow would have enough time to dedicate to a start-up and raising a child. Especially as a single parent. That's cold."

"That's bullshit," Lauder said, sending a hard stare out

the tinted glass. How many kids had been denied a loving home because of BS like this? *The system has to change.*

"Whoa."

This drew Lauder's attention back to Chuck. What had he uncovered now? And could it be any more devastating than the adoption news? "What?"

Chuck waved him off. "Nothing. I just didn't realize she used clay and skeletal remains—namely, a skull— to recreate what a person looked like. A *deceased* person," he said, as if the skull hadn't been a giveaway. "It's kind of eerie."

Lauder shook his head at his friend, then turned his attention back out the window. He couldn't explain why, but his urge, his need to get close to Willow was greater than ever.

Willow preferred clay over people. Clay didn't disappoint. It simply remained there in one big clump allowing you to manipulate it in any manner you wanted, not the other way around. Clay didn't work you like men.

A vision of Lauder's handsome face burned into her thoughts, and she gritted her teeth. Her best friend, Hannah, stood next to her and laughed, pulling her from the offending image.

"Um, sweetie, everything okay?" Hannah asked.

"Perfect. Why do you ask?" Willow said without looking at her friend.

"Because instead of John Doe, you've sculpted a Nubian god. One that looks very familiar."

"Huh?" Willow eyed her work and gasped. "Oh, God." How had she... She groaned. It had been two weeks since she'd seen Lauder. Why couldn't she stop thinking about him?

"Who is it?" Hannah asked, scrutinizing the form.

Willow sighed heavily, debating whether or not to go into details. Deciding it might help her rid the thoughts of Lauder, she said, "Remember the guy I told you about? The one from Drip Drop?"

"Dude from your past?"

Willow nodded, then fanned her hand toward the chunk of clay she'd unconsciously molded into Lauder's likeness. "Meet Lauder Tolson."

Hannah's cinnamon-colored eyes widened, awareness apparently setting in. "*Senatorial candidate* Lauder Tolson?"

Willow wiped her hands down the front of her brown apron. "Yep, that's the one."

"Oh, my good Lord. Lauder Tolson is your ex? *The* Lauder Tolson?"

"He's not my ex. He—"

"Deflowered you." Hannah grinned.

Heat warmed Willow's neck and rose to her cheeks. "Yeah, that." Willow thought back to her sixteenth birthday and the bold, shaky words she'd said to Lauder. *I want to do it. I want to do it with you.* The lopsided smile Lauder had flashed right before he'd kissed her senseless mimicked the one she'd created on his clay face.

Lauder had spoken the truth at the coffee shop. She hadn't always hated him. That had happened when he'd taken her virginity and then told all of his friends. Then had the nerve to adamantly deny it—more like lie—to her face.

Hannah started again, drawing Willow's attention.

Reaching for the piece, Hannah said, "Well, the brother is fine. If you don't want him, I'll gladly take him."

Willow swatted Hannah away, surprised by her protectiveness over the bust. How in hell had she managed to sculpt an entire bust of Lauder without realizing it?

This man was too much in her head, too potent in her thoughts. She had to stop thinking about him. But how, when his presence had opened a cavern of old memories? Some good, some not so good.

"Don't let the strong jaw and perfect bone structure fool you. He's the Antichrist," Willow said, staring at the figure as if it were speaking to her. She felt like punching it in the face; however, since it was some of her best work, she refrained. But at that moment, she vowed to never think about Lauder Tolson again.

"Um, Willow?"

"Mmm-hmm."

"You might want to cover the Antichrist."

Cover him? Hannah was being overdramatic. Lauder wasn't that dang tempting. Willow tilted her head to one side and studied the sculpture. Actually, he was. Even in clay form, the man was beautiful. *Ugh. Never thinking about him again*, she reminded herself.

Lauder did foolish things to her system. Sinfully delicious things. Things that got her juices flowing. She made a mental note to call Reggie, her occasional friend with benefits. She needed his benefits tonight. That would help rid her system of Lauder Tolson.

"I don't think covering him is necessary," Willow said. "Now, had you said toss him in the trash, I could have supported that."

"Nah, you should probably cover it. Apparently, someone left the gates of hell open. And look what just escaped. I might just be willing to sacrifice salvation for a night with that delicious devil."

Willow glanced over her shoulder just as Lauder was being directed toward them. "What the hell—" She gasped. "No way."

She frantically looked for something to conceal her rendition of him.

"Use your apron," Hannah said out the side of her mouth.

Good idea. Willow fiddled with the strings. "Shoot. I can't get it untied."

"Oh, yeah. He wants you, Will. Look at how he's undressing you with his eyes. He wants to blow your back completely out. And judging by those long, muscular legs, he could do just that. Lawd, I love a man in a tailored suit."

Glancing up caused Willow to lose valuable time. Mainly because watching Lauder float toward them stalled her brain. As she raked her eyes over him, her stomach fluttered. Why did she keep responding to him?

Out of time, Willow blocked clay Lauder with her body as the real thing strolled inside the room. The idea that clay Lauder was staring at her ass made things even more awkward. What had she done to the universe to deserve such a disturbance in her life as Lauder?

One good thing came from Lauder's approach. It shut Hannah up. When he nodded at Hannah, Willow thought the woman would split the corners of her mouth smiling so hard. *Shameless*, Willow thought until Lauder slid his gaze to her. The mild sensations she'd experienced moments ago blossomed into full-fledged lust convulsions.

"Willow."

Lauder's tone was so damn smooth, so damn steady, so damn confident one would think she'd actually invited him to invade her space. "Lauder." Nope, her tone wasn't smooth. Probably couldn't be considered steady. Definitely wasn't confident. But at least she'd managed not to moan. A triumph in her book. Small, but a win nonetheless.

When Lauder's eyes lowered to her lips, a bout of nervous tension knotted her stomach. Why was he eyeballing her mouth? Her eyes were what he should have been focused on. They were the only things he would ever connect to.

Lauder's eyes rose, and his lips curled slightly. "I found you."

"I wasn't lost."

"We've all been lost at one point in our lives. Sometimes, we don't even realize we're waiting to be found."

Willow's eyes narrowed at him. *What in hell does that mean?* She didn't bother asking him to elaborate, because she wasn't interested in his cryptic logic.

"I really hope these sprinklers work," Hannah said, eyeing overhead.

Willow scowled at her friend.

Hannah visually attempted to bite back a smile. "I'm going to give you two some priv—"

Willow's scowl deepened, warning her against leaving the room.

"Like I said, I'll be right over here." Hannah pointed over her shoulder and backed away.

Refocusing on Lauder, Willow tried not to pay attention to how good he smelled. Like mature, sexy man. "What are you doing here?"

"I wanted to see you."

She folded her arms across her chest. "Why?"

"Because you're nice to look at."

Hannah made some ridiculous sound that drew both their attentions. Yep, the woman was fired as her best friend. Although, she could admit—only to herself—that he was pleasant on the eyes, too.

"Well, thank you for stopping by to look at me, but I want to do you."

Willow's body went board stiff. There were a hundred ways she could have responded to her word blunder: sprint from the room like she was on fire, fake a blackout, slide a heated glance in an audibly tickled Hannah's direction. Instead, her gaze remained pinned to Lauder's. She straightened her spine, because that's what a lady in complete control did. And she was in complete control. Completely.

Clearing her throat, she said, "I apologize. What I meant to say was I have *work* to do. I should show you out."

Not bothering to wait for his response, she took off toward the door. Hannah's warning—a sharp gasp—came a fraction too late. Willow realized the mistake she'd made.

"Huh. Damn, you are good with your hands."

Lauder said it as if he'd discussed her abilities with someone. Again, straightening her spine, because that's what a lady in— Oh, hell. Who was she kidding? She wasn't in control. Hadn't been since Lauder crashed into her world again. The best she could do was to pretend his presence had no effect on her.

Backtracking to join real Lauder staring at clay Lauder, she said, "I can explain that."

"Oh, this should be good," Hannah said just loud enough for Willow to hear.

Lauder lifted one of his large hands. For a brief second, a memory of how his hands used to explore her body—slowly, cautiously, thoroughly—played in her head. *Stop it*, she warned her defiant brain.

"No need. Obviously, you think I'm nice to look at, too," Lauder said.

Willow barked a laugh. "Don't flatter yourself. There's a perfectly good explanation for this."

Lauder folded his arms across his chest, causing his

biceps to mushroom against the steel blue shirt he wore. The sight was like a magnet, and her eyes were drawn to it. At seventeen, his arms hadn't been puny, but they hadn't been sculpted like this, either. Clearly, he spent a lot of time in the gym.

"Okay. So…" Lauder said.

"So, what?" she said absently.

"So, what is the explanation?"

Willow released a nervous chuckle, sobered, then laughed. "I'm a forensic sculptor. This is what I do. I sculpt people."

"Oh, I get that. But why did you sculpt me?"

Stay cool. You've got this. Don't let him shake you. Play it cool. "Oh, you…you thought that was you?" Okay, so playing dumb was probably not the best strategy.

Lauder narrowed his eyes at her, then slid them to the clay, then back to her. "That's not me?"

"No."

He chuckled a sound so smooth and sexy, it caressed her skin, causing fine bumps to prickle her skin.

"That's not me?" he asked a second time.

"I said no."

Lauder nodded once. "Huh." A second later, he glanced in Hannah's direction. "Excuse me? Can you come over and help me out a second?"

What was he up to? Hannah joined them in front of the sculpture, visibly just as confused as Willow was.

"Lauder Tolson, by the way." He offered Hannah his hand.

Another toothy smile spread across Hannah's face. "Oh, I know who you are. Hannah Burrows. Nice to meet you."

"Same here. So, Hannah, does this excellent work of art resemble me?"

Willow held her breath as Hannah scrutinized real Lauder, then the clay version. She tilted her head to the right, then to the left. A second later, she pressed her index finger into her chin.

"There is a strong resemblance. Especially here in the jaw region." She used her finger to point out the area. "But I don't think it looks exactly like you. If you hold your head just right, I guess it could pass for your distant cousin."

Lauder burst into laughter. "My distant cousin?" He laughed some more. "Okay, I get it. Some kind of woman-code thing going on."

Willow smirked. Hannah was definitely rehired. Eyeing Lauder, she said, "Now that we have that mystery solved, I'm guessing we can move forward." Finally getting her apron unknotted, she tossed it over clay Lauder. "I'll toss it in the garbage later."

Lauder unapologetically checked her out. His scrutiny diminished some of the confidence Hannah's flawless performance had given her.

Finding her eyes again, Lauder flashed one of those lopsided smiles he'd clearly perfected over the years. "Will you have dinner with me tonight?"

"Yes," Hannah said, answering for Willow. "Um, I'll be over…yeah." A second later, she was gone.

"So? Dinner?" Lauder said.

"No."

"*No.* Wow." He massaged his jaw as if she'd slapped him. "Just like that? You sure you don't need a few minutes to pretend to consider it?"

"There's nothing to consider. You asked me a question, I gave you an answer."

"The wrong answer."

"In your opinion."

"Reconsider."

"I have plans tonight."

"A date?"

"None of your business."

"How about tomorrow night? Or the night after?"

Why did he seem so determined? And was she actually contemplating a yes in her head? Clearly, his delicious scent had made her delirious. "I'm busy for the foreseeable future." She shrugged. "Work. I'm sure you know how it is."

Lauder studied her for a long moment. "Well, if you're busy, you're busy." He flashed a half smile, then turned toward Hannah. "It was nice meeting you, Hannah."

"Same here. And you have my vote. Edmondson is a joke."

"I agree. Thanks for the vote. I appreciate that."

Willow rolled her eyes at the unnecessary charm Lauder dripped all over the place. *Just leave already.*

"I hope you enjoy the rest of your day, Willow." He started away, but stopped. "Oh. Here's my business card. Just in case you change your mind."

Willow took the wedge with a smile, then watched Lauder glide away like a sexy jaguar. Damn, he should really come with a warning label. Hannah came to stand next to her and shook her head. "What?"

"I can't believe you lied to that fine, fine specimen of a man like that."

"I didn't lie. I am busy. With work…and other stuff."

"You should have asked him to escort you to the A Hope for Home fund-raiser. With that sexy beast on your arm, every eye in the place would be on you."

"I don't want every eye in the place on me. I prefer blending into the background."

"Remaining in the background is going to be kind of hard as a senator's significant other."

Willow whipped her head toward Hannah. "I'm not a senator's significant anything." She glanced back in time enough to see the elevator doors close, freeing her from Lauder's spellbinding presence.

Hannah laughed. "You don't even see it, do you?"

Willow turned back to Hannah. "See what?"

Hannah pinched Willow's cheeks like a little old lady did a child. "Your cluelessness is just so adorable," she said in a voice reserved for babies. "Honey, does Lauder Tolson strike you as a man who would give up that easily? He's coming for you, sweetie." She rested her hands on Willow's shoulders. "I suggest you prepare to be conquered."

Willow wanted to protest, tell Hannah she was insane. Unfortunately, she, too, had the feeling she hadn't seen the last of Lauder. *Prepare to be conquered?* Ha! Lauder would never get close enough to conquer her. And that she could guarantee.

Chapter 3

For the life of her, Willow couldn't figure out why she'd agreed to spend her Saturday night mingling with total strangers. Why hadn't she gone with her first instinct and simply written a check to show her support for A Hope for Home Foundation like she typically did?

Hannah, Willow grumbled to herself. Her friend had given her this long, drawn-out speech about how getting out once in a while was good for the soul. Hannah was always giving her speeches, so why had she chosen tonight of all nights to listen?

The gnawing in her gut that urged her to come, she reminded herself. Next time, she'd just take an antacid and go to bed.

Maybe she could slip out as quietly as she'd slipped in, climb back into her vehicle and hightail it back across town. Sipping an ice-cold glass of grape punch in her T-shirt and panties sounded really good right about now.

Just as she made her mind up to leave, she spotted Gloria Barrett—organizer of this fine affair—headed her way. *Shoot.* She'd never get away now.

In her early sixties, Gloria could easily pass for a woman twenty years younger. With her caramel skin, curves most twenty-year-olds would die for and dazzling gray eyes, she had men flocking to her. But ask anyone and they'd tell you her heart belonged to one man and one man only, her husband of over three decades, Patrick Barrett.

"Willow. You made it." Gloria snatched her into a tight hug, then held her at arm's length. "You look amazing. Hon, you're going to get some of these married men in trouble with this figure-hugging number here. And that deep teal color… Gorgeous."

Willow ironed a hand down the front of the satiny full-length gown. "Thank you. Just something I threw together." Which was a lie because she'd spent a month searching every evening-gown site on the internet until she'd finally found something that caught her eye. The sleeveless dress had cost her a pretty penny, but when she'd scrutinized herself in the mirror, she was convinced it had been totally worth the expense.

"Come with me. I have someone I want to introduce you to. Plus, I'm sure he'd appreciate us saving him from those lust-filled vultures circling him."

Willow didn't get the chance to protest before Gloria had her halfway across the floor of the large ballroom. With all of the positive energy in the stylishly decorated space, Willow considered being here not such a bad thing after all. And it was for a good cause. Two hours of her Saturday night wouldn't kill her.

Besides, it wasn't like she would have been painting the town red anyway. Inwardly, she sighed, agreeing with Hannah's frequent piece of advice. *I have got to get a life.* One good thing about being here, it kept her mind off—

Willow gasped. *Lauder? What is he doing here?*

Something ridiculous crossed her mind. Had he known she'd be there? No. How would he?

Willow's eyes raked over him. If Hannah thought he

looked scrumptious when he'd visited their office, the woman's mouth would be watering now. Dressed in all black, with the top button of his shirt unfastened, he was so alluring that it was sickening.

She gnawed at the corner of her lip. It made no sense for one man to be so damn gorgeous. Even his body language—sure, confident, relaxed—made him attractive. While there were plenty of handsome men in attendance, Lauder was in a category all his very own. Obviously, she wasn't the only woman affected by his magnetism. He practically had a harem of women surrounding him.

"Just look at him. Getting every panty in the room soaking wet," Gloria said in a hushed tone.

Gloria was a mix of a prim and proper socialite and an unfiltered comedian. Judging by the dreamy-eyed women clinging to Lauder's every word, Gloria was right about the panty thing. Willow didn't want to be a casualty of whatever drug he was dispensing. But before she could devise an escape plan, Lauder slid his dangerously dark and daunting gaze in her direction.

The intensity of their connection caused her lips to part slightly, a stream of heated air escaping. She refused to label it a searing line of suppressed desire. Swallowing hard, she fought the need to turn away. *And let Lauder think he had an effect on me? No way.*

The faint furrow of his brow suggested he was just as surprised to see her as she'd been to see him. The straight line of his tempting lips slowly curled into a tantalizing smile. His intense scrutiny felt like delicate kisses feathering her skin. Just the thought of his mouth on her caused the space between her legs to tingle.

Why? She hadn't known his touch in close to twenty years.

"Excuse me, ladies. Might I steal this handsome creature for a moment?" Gloria threaded her arm through Lauder's and led him away. "Lauder, sweetie, between you and this pretty lady right here, y'all are going to cause a riot in here."

Willow could feel Lauder's eyes on her, but this time she refused to look in his direction.

"Lauder Tolson—future Senator Tolson—I'd like you to meet—"

"Willow Dawson," Lauder said.

Gloria glanced from Lauder to Willow. "You two know each other?"

"Um…yes. We, um, we knew each other once. When we were younger." Willow felt as if she were a specimen in a petri dish being scrutinized for the slightest change in composition.

Gloria smiled. "I see. Well, Lauder is one of the most generous contributors to A Hope for Home. And he donated one of his warehouses for us to use as a staging location."

"Wow. A modern-day Robin Hood," Willow said. Instantly, she regretted sounding so patronizing.

Gloria started to speak, but someone summoned her. "Excuse me. Got to go earn these zeros," she said. "I'll leave you two to catch up with one another."

A beat of awkward silence lingered between Willow and Lauder. At least, awkward for her because his eyes fixed on her as if trying to read her mind. Oh, he really didn't want to read her thoughts right now.

Deciding she'd be the bigger person, she said, "The Robin Hood comment… I didn't mean to sound so—"

"Condescending?"

"Yes." Another string of silence played between them, Lauder's gaze never leaving her. "A Hope for Home is a

great organization. How long have you been involved?"
she asked.

"Since its inception, so a little over two years. Gloria
can be very convincing, but when she told me the foundation intended to furnish the first permanent home for
foster youth who'd aged out of the system, she had me.
I'm too familiar with the struggle of trying to survive
after foster care."

The sadness that flashed in Lauder's eyes stirred Willow's curiosity. Had he gone through something? If he
had, he'd clearly gotten through it okay.

"I usually never attend these things," Lauder said.

They had that in common. Not that she was keeping
a tally. "So how did you end up here tonight?"

"Something drew me here."

A similar thing had happened to her, but she would
never in a hundred years share that with him. The smile
melted from Willow's face, her stomach fluttering from
the way Lauder eyed her. Was he insinuating she had
led him here? How ridiculous. Lines like that probably
worked on his other women, but it wouldn't work on her.
"Uh-huh. Well, if you'll excuse me."

Lauder flashed a half smile and gave a single nod. "It
was nice seeing you again."

Willow walked away without mirroring his sentiment,
because it wasn't nice seeing him again. In fact, she'd
prefer to never see him again. Unfortunately, he seemed
to keep popping up.

Not wanting Lauder to believe he'd run her off, she
forced herself to stay at the event a little while longer.
Despite her attempts to maintain a safe distance from the
man who made her body hum, everywhere she turned
Lauder was there. *Looking like a ripe apple straight out
of temptation's orchard.*

Was she crazy or did he seem determined to be near her? The fact that she found the idea faintly endearing angered her. What was he doing to her? And why in hell was she allowing it?

Lauder joined her at one of the fabric-draped highboy tables. "If we keep bumping into each other like this, I'm going to call it fate."

"Oh, yeah? Well, some people would call it stalking." She flashed a low-wattage smile.

He laughed a sweet, sexy sound that made her stomach quiver. *Why?* Why couldn't she simply ignore him? Ignore his delicious scent, those hypnotizing eyes, that gobble-you-all-the-way-up mouth, the way he filled out that suit. What kind of sorcery was this man? Shaking some sense into herself, she dispelled the idea he'd cast some sort of seduction curse on her.

"Do you want to get out of here? Grab a coffee or dessert or something?"

Willow glanced to the overabundance of desserts on the long table several feet away, then to the coffee bar next to it. Eyeing Lauder again, she said, "I should really get home. I have—" she searched the depths of her brain "—church in the morning. Early in the morning. Like seven o'clock." Lying on the Lord. Yep, she'd just secured herself a nice, hot front-row seat in hell. "Good night, Lauder."

When she turned to leave, Lauder captured her arm. She gasped at the onset of tiny lightning bolts striking through her system. The raw intensity of his touch overtook her. And had she not placed a hand on the table, she was sure she would have toppled over.

Lauder's tone was gentle when he spoke. "Willow, wait."

He was in luck. She couldn't budge, despite desperately wanting to sprint away from him, from this—the insanely powerful connection that had her rooted to the floor. Maybe he was the energy she'd felt earlier. Not the entire room. Just one man.

Drawing in a deep breath, she spoke over her shoulder. "What do you want, Lauder?"

"You."

That was the last answer in the world she'd expected and not one she wanted to hear.

It was a long while before Willow turned to face him, but when she did, Lauder could tell he'd stunned her. Hell, he'd stunned himself. Yes, he'd been thinking the word *you*, just hadn't meant to say it aloud. Or had he?

Truth be told, he did want her. Wanted her in the best and worst ways imaginable. Wanted to yank her into his arms and kiss her like a madman. Wanted to strip her out of that curve-hugging dress that made the sexually deprived beast inside him ravenous with desire. Wanted to explore every inch of her with his tongue. Wanted to taste and savor her essence. And after all of that, he wanted to make slow, passionate love to her. All. Night. Long.

But right now, he had to push that want aside and focus on need. He needed her, because like he'd told Chuckie, no other woman would do. Seeing her tonight, experiencing this unexplainable tug toward her, made his desire to get close to her even more urgent.

Confusion replaced the shock on Willow's beautiful face. A thousand scenarios had to be rushing through her head. At least she hadn't taken off across the room. She seemed pretty good at running. Mainly from him.

"Can we talk?" he said, holding out his hand for her to take.

Willow eyed his hand like it was a snake that would strike if she made the slightest of moves. Apparently, she determined the serpent wasn't poisonous because she slid her trembling palm against his. Why was she so nervous?

His palm sizzled from her touch. He clasped his fingers around her delicate flesh and led her from the crowded and noisy ballroom. Passing the bay of public elevators, they ventured to the private one that would take them to his residence located on the upper level of the De Lore Hotel.

Willow didn't budge when the door opened. Reclaiming her hand, she stared at him as if she were totally confused by what was happening.

"Where are we going?" Her tone was quiet and guarded.

"To my place."

"You live in a hotel?"

That seemed to concern her more than the fact that he was leading her there. He nodded. "The upper levels are residential."

"Oh."

When the elevator doors started to close, Lauder stepped between them. "We can talk here if you'd prefer." He didn't want to scare her off.

After a second or two, Willow shook her head and brushed past him. Lauder pressed the button, and the doors closed. The ride to the twentieth floor was a quiet one. He used the time to admire how damn gorgeous Willow looked. Her hair was in a tight bun positioned on the top of her head, exposing that neck he craved to lick, nip and kiss.

Her sweet scent filled the close space. The fragrance only made him want her more.

Inside his place Willow surveyed her surroundings before moving to the floor-to-ceiling window and staring out. "This is a fantastic view."

Lauder shrugged off his suit coat and joined her.

"Thanks." He studied her profile, unapologetically admiring the woman she'd become. Being here with Willow felt right to him. Too right. She'd taken him completely off guard. No woman had ever roused him like this one. At seventeen and now.

A beat of silence passed.

"Why am I here, Lauder?" she asked, never sliding her eyes away from the glow of downtown Raleigh.

Lauder inched his hands into his pockets. "I need your help."

Willow's head slowly turned toward him, uncertainty dancing on her pretty face. "My help?"

"Let's sit," he said, resting his hand on the small of her back and leading her to the sofa.

For the next several minutes, Lauder explained everything to Willow. He couldn't read the stony expression on her face. Was she considering his proposal or thinking he was crazy as hell?

Then out of the blue, she laughed. This wasn't a ha-ha-you're-funny kind of laugh. It was a struggle-to-catch-your-breath, aching-sides, belly roll.

"You're not serious," she said between fits.

Lauder leaned forward and rested his elbows on his thighs. "As a heart attack."

Willow's amusement dried up, and she eyed him with a gaped mouth. "There are a thousand women who I'm sure would jump at the opportunity to play your love interest." Her brow furrowed. "Why me?"

He shrugged. "We have history." Maybe not the best, but history nonetheless. *And chemistry.* But he kept that part to himself. She didn't need him to point out something he was sure she felt, too. Such a potent attraction was hard to ignore or deny.

"Huh." Her gaze slid away. "I'm not…" Her words trailed off. "No. I can't—"

"I know this is a lot to process. Don't answer now. Take some time to think about it. This could benefit the both of us."

She whipped her head toward him. "How in the world could this possibly benefit me?"

He debated whether or not to mention what Chuck had told him about her adoption attempts, but deciding it would help strengthen his case, he said, "I know you're trying to adopt."

Willow pushed her brows together. "Should I even bother asking how you know this?"

"It doesn't matter, Willow. All that matters is I may be able to help." Lauder could see her mulling his words over in her head. To sweeten the deal, he added, "There are perks to dating a politician," and hoped she'd agree.

"You're okay with deceiving your constituents?" She gave a single, humorless laugh. "Of course you are. You wouldn't have approached me with this if you weren't."

Chuck's passionate argument had persuaded Lauder to go along with this needing-a-girlfrend-to-improve-his-image charade, but the judgment present in Willow's voice made him question whether or not he'd done the right thing. Standing, he moved back to the window. "Do a little harm to perform a lot of good," he mumbled more to himself.

"What?"

Lauder turned to Willow. "Nothing." Sliding his hands into his pockets, he said, "I have big plans for this state, Willow. Including the foster care system. *Especially* the foster care system. A system that failed you. A system that failed me. A system that's still failing kids every single day. You have seen this firsthand." Offering his hand, he said, "I'll escort you back downstairs."

She ignored his outstretched arm. "I can find my own way."

It was evident she was attempting to escape him, so he didn't protest. A second later, she was gone. And he doubted he would ever hear from her again.

Chapter 4

Willow hadn't slept well for the past two days. Every time she placed her head on the pillow and closed her eyes, Lauder's handsome face filled her thoughts, along with the ridiculous request he'd made. Pretend to be his significant other. *For votes.*

Clearly, he hadn't changed all that much. The same old deceptive Lauder Tolson, just in larger and more exquisite packaging. She punched the mound of clay she'd been working on, chastising herself for finding him so attractive and being unable to ignore the intense chemistry between them.

"Uh-oh. Whenever you knead clay like that, all rough and barbarian-like, you're upset," Hannah said, moving up behind Willow.

Willow hadn't shared with Hannah the conversation she'd had with Lauder. Not because she didn't trust her best friend with the information, but because she was still in shock by it herself. "It's nothing."

"Out with it."

Willow really didn't want to discuss it, but on the other hand, she did. She needed to vent to someone about just how insane this all was. She sighed and faced Hannah.

"Total secrecy." It was something they said when what would follow had to be taken to the grave.

"I understand," Hannah replied.

Willow spent the next twenty minutes telling the story as it had been told to her. Including the part about them both benefitting from this ludicrous scheme. At the end, she waited for Hannah to burst out laughing just as she had. Nothing.

"And you said no?" Hannah said.

"Of course I did. This proposition is insane. I won't get caught up in his web of deceit."

"Let's discuss the pros and cons of such an arrangement."

She must have been nuts for even entertaining Hannah, but she sighed and nodded.

"Con: you'd have to give up this thing with Reggie. But if he's as lousy in bed as you claim he is, that shouldn't be much of a hardship."

"He's not lousy in bed. He's just…unadventurous."

Hannah grinned. "I bet Lauder is plenty adventurous." She bounced her brows twice. "Anyway, severing ties with Reggie might not be such a bad thing. It could definitely be a pro."

Reggie was familiar. They both got what they wanted, then went their separate ways, until they needed more. Out of curiosity, Willow inquired, "Why?"

"Because he's falling for you."

Willow laughed. "What? No, he's not. Reggie and I are just friends with occasional benefits."

"You may not see it, because 'just friends' is what you agreed to, but he has a thing for you."

Could Hannah actually be right? Was Reggie falling for her? The idea might have put a smile on most women's faces. Not hers. She didn't want any arrangement she couldn't easily walk away from. She didn't do attachments. In her mind, they exposed you to potential heartbreak. Something she'd had far too much of in her life.

Hannah's words broke into Willow's racing thoughts. "Lauder was right, you know? There could be a major perk to dating him."

"Like what?"

"Your adoption application. Or have you forgotten about that?"

Of course she hadn't. It always lingered in the forefront of her thoughts. Waiting for that call revealing whether or not she'd be allowed to give a child the love she'd never had was daily torture. "No, I haven't forgotten. You know I want to adopt a child more than anything in this world."

"Lauder's proposition could be the answer. A senatorial candidate has clout."

For the first time, Lauder's proposal had her attention. But it only lasted briefly. "I don't agree with what he's doing."

"But we can agree that it's not the worst thing in the world. If it's not you, babe, it'll be someone else."

For some crazy reason, the idea of another woman playing the role she'd been handpicked for troubled her more than it should. Actually, it shouldn't have bothered her at all.

"Who would you rather see win, Edmondson or that fine, fine chocolate Lauder Tolson?"

That was an easy one. Edmondson was a joke, parading around town with his robotic family, when everyone knew he didn't care one iota about improving anyone's life but his own. "Lauder, of course, but—"

"But nothing. It's settled. You're doing this. For the

good of your fellow voters of this state. And the precious child who's going to have the most amazing mother in the whole wide world." Hannah hugged Willow, then held her at arm's length. "Now repeat after me: *I'm going to do this.*"

Willow bit at the corner of her lip, still unconvinced that this was a road she wanted to travel. Hannah had made valid points, but there were risks involved with playing Lauder's pretend lover. So many risks. Clearly, there was a real attraction between them. Could she actually spend extended amounts of time with him and not fall prey to his charm?

"Say it," Hannah continued. "Say, *I'm going to do this.*"

After several moments, Willow mumbled under her breath.

"What was that? I didn't hear you."

"I'm going to do this," she said, the declaration feeling like the kiss of doom.

Lauder hadn't expected Willow's impromptu visit, especially since he hadn't had any contact with her for close to a week. Now here she stood, mere feet from him and looking like the gold at the end of a rainbow. He played it cool, but all he wanted to do was yank her against his chest, sweep an arm across his desk, gently place Willow on top of it and bury himself inside her.

Unfortunately, none of that would happen. However, his aching body certainly wished it would.

"Willow? What a pleasant surprise." He eased onto the edge of his desk and folded his arms across his chest. "It's nice to—"

"I'll allow you to use me, but I'm going to use you in return," she said, her expression void of emotion.

Use her? Was that what she thought he wanted to do?

Lauder massaged the side of his face, needing a second to recover from her words. Actually, as harsh as it sounded, it was exactly what he was doing, but she then intended to benefit from him, too. "And how will you use me, Willow?" He could think of several ways he would have liked for the usage to occur, none of them suitable to mention aloud. But every one of them stirred him below the waist.

"You were correct. I do want to adopt a child. But I don't want any unfair advantage," Willow continued.

Unfair advantage. Had that been meant to be a jab? "I see. So what do you need from me?"

"I don't *need* anything from you, Lauder. What I *want* is for you to put in a good word for me when the time comes."

Obviously, she had a distorted definition of the term *unfair advantage*, because her request fell snugly within those perimeters. However, he allowed her to continue to believe otherwise. She seemed set on riding her high horse until the thing died of exhaustion.

Deciding to make her sweat a bit, he said, "I don't think this will work, Willow."

"May I ask why?"

Lauder braced a hand on either side of the desk. "For us to be convincing as a couple, we would actually need to like one another. Now, I like you plenty, but you act as if you can't bear the sight of me." He shrugged. "It won't—"

Before he could finish the thought, Willow was between his legs, her arms wrapped around his neck and lips locked to his. The sensation that shot to his groin nearly toppled him off the desk's edge.

The kiss was unhurried and sensual.

Profound and thorough.

Hot and delicious.

Absolutely perfect.

Willow's tongue probed the inside of his mouth without hesitation. She tasted sweet, like grape candy. Lip gloss, maybe. When his brain finally rebooted, he responded to their intimate connection, enveloping his arms around her warm body and holding her close to him.

He wanted her.

Desperately needed her.

Willow's tense frame relaxed against him, and he held her a little more lightly. He wanted this moment to last forever. Unfortunately, several sizzling seconds later, the pleasure came to an abrupt end with Willow pulling away. She ran the pad of her thumb across his bottom lip, then stared him square in the eyes.

"I trust that was convincing enough."

Like a deer trapped in the headlights of a big rig, he couldn't speak or move. All he could do was gape into her dazzling eyes.

"I'll take that as a yes."

He didn't miss the smugness in her tone. A beat later, she freed herself from his hold and moved toward the door like a sexy siren. His eyes fixed on her ample behind in those figure-flattering jeans. His manhood throbbed so hard, he had to adjust himself. *Oh, you will pay for this in the most sensual manner possible.*

Blame it on ego, but Lauder couldn't allow her to get away believing she had the upper hand—despite the fact that she did have it. Pushing to a full stand, he said, "We're going to need to spend some time together. Get to know each other." He already knew one thing about her for sure…she was one hell of a kisser.

Willow stopped at the door, her hand resting on the knob. Over her shoulder, she said, "This Saturday. Six o'clock."

Opening the door, she was gone.

Lauder chuckled and massaged his jaw. He wasn't sure what, but Willow was doing something to his guarded heart. What was worse, he liked it.

Returning behind his desk, he dropped into the plush office chair, rested his elbow on the armrest and gingerly glided two fingers across his bottom lip. The next time their lips touched—and there would be a next time—he would be the one in control.

Two taps sounded at his door, and Lauder grew overly excited. Had Willow returned? "Come in." A smile lit his face, then melted away. "Oh, it's just you," he said to his foster brother Roth Lexington.

"Damn. Should I leave and come back?"

Lauder rounded his desk. "Nah, man. I just thought you were someone else."

The two exchanged an affectionate hug. Though he and Roth weren't related, people actually thought they were biological brothers because they favored each other so much. Both over six feet tall, both had deep brown skin tones, both had prominent features and a commanding presence.

"Where's Alonso? I thought he was rolling with us to lunch," Lauder said.

Roth chuckled. "He's going to meet us there. Had to go home and kiss the twins and do only God knows what to Vivian."

The room filled with laughter.

"Man, looking at you and Lo, I can almost picture myself settling down. Wife, kids, white picket fence. Almost."

"It's the best feeling in the world, man, to come home to a wife and kids you love more than the sun."

Lauder enjoyed seeing Roth so happy. He was a good brother and deserved all the happiness life had to give.

"What about that sister who nearly plowed into me rushing from your office? Does she have anything to do with your change of heart? Last I recall, you said you're never getting married and definitely not having any kids."

"Willow Dawson," Lauder said, dropping into the chair across from his desk.

Roth occupied the opposite one. "Willow Dawson?" His brow furrowed. "Why does that name sound so familiar?" Obviously, it dawned on him. "Wait, is she the same Willow Dawson who got you kicked out of the group home years ago?"

Lauder couldn't believe Roth still remembered that. Though he shouldn't have been surprised. Roth had the memory of an elephant. "One and the same."

To be honest, Willow hadn't gotten him kicked out of the group home; breaking Marvin Kramer's nose had gotten him kicked out. But Lauder had been defending Willow's honor, so he guessed she could share some of the blame. One day he'd get around to sharing the details of his honor brawl with her. Maybe if she knew the truth, she'd drop her grudge against him.

Roth cut into Lauder's thoughts.

"Are you two…"

Lauder hadn't told Roth about Willow playing his pretend lover, but knew he could trust the man with the information. "Chuck thought I should come across as more family oriented, so I've enlisted Willow to play my make-believe lover."

Lauder studied Roth's face for any signs of disapproval. There was none that he could spot.

Roth chuckled. "Are you sure it's all make-believe?

The woman has you thinking about settling down. That's...huge. Especially for you."

Lauder rubbed his jaw. "Can I ask you something?"

"Shoot."

"How'd you learn to trust Tressa?" Lauder figured that if Roth could open himself up to another person, as guarded as he'd always been, anyone could.

"It wasn't easy. But when my trust issues jeopardized my relationship with Tress, I vowed to change. I knew that woman was my forever. I didn't want to lose her."

"How did you know she was the one?"

Roth beamed as if reliving a beautiful memory, then in a flash sobered. "Her touch."

By the intense expression on his face, Lauder assumed there was more to the touch story than Roth was sharing. He didn't pry.

"You'll know," Roth said, standing. "Now let's go. I'm starving."

Lauder scrubbed a hand over his head. Thing was, he was sure he already knew. And knowing complicated things.

Chapter 5

"You did what!" Hannah's bright eyes glowed with excitement.

Willow flailed her arms in Hannah's direction. *"Shhh,"* she warned, coming from behind her desk to close her office door. "Keep your voice down." Willow peeped out to make sure no one was within earshot of them, then pushed the door shut. Facing Hannah, she rested a hand on her forehead and sighed heavily. "I kissed him. Like, *really* kissed him. I couldn't stop kissing him."

The second her lips touched Lauder's it was like she'd had an out-of-body experience, as if she were hovering high above watching herself kiss Lauder, unable to stop. By the time she'd pulled away, her body was so electrified she thought the current would kill her.

"Was it good?" Hannah asked.

Willow attempted to bite back a smile, but it broke through. "It was fantastic."

Hannah squealed. "Yes! I knew it. I knew you still had feelings for him. After all of these years apart, your heart still beats for your first." She cupped her hands under her chin and went all dreamy eyed. "That's so romantic."

"Because I enjoyed a spine-tingling kiss way more

than I should have doesn't mean I'm still in love with
Lauder Tolson. It's been—" Willow paused, noting the
odd look on Hannah's face. "What?"

"Still?"

"What?"

"You said *still* in love with him. Meaning, at one point,
you were in love with him."

Willow released a shaky laugh and rubbed her shoulder. "I—I was sixteen. Of course I thought I was in love.
Isn't that what sixteen-year-old girls do? Fall recklessly
in love with bad boys?"

"Yes, reckless sixteen-year-olds. Since we met fresh-
man year of college, you've always been ordered, in control, methodical."

Never been reckless? Then how did Hannah explain
her agreeing to play Lauder's fake lover? In her opinion,
that was as reckless as you could get. She reminded herself why she was doing it. The idea of becoming a mother
made her decision less daunting.

Hannah smiled. "How long have we known each
other?"

"Over ten—"

"Yep, over ten years," Hannah said, cutting Willow
off. "So I know when you're lying. Even when you're not
rubbing the brown off your shoulder."

Willow allowed her arm to fall to her side. "I'm not—"

Hannah pinched Willow's lips together. *"Shush."*

Willow protested in an array of grunts.

"Shush," Hannah repeated. "Are you listening?"

Defeated, Willow nodded her head. "Mmm-hmm."

"Good. Let this thing between you and Lauder happen.
You deserve a man like Lauder—fine as hell, rich and
powerful. You deserve great sex—the kind that leaves

you hobbling afterwards. And you definitely deserve love—the kind of love that will last an eternity."

Willow hummed *but*.

"*Shush.* You're going to go on your date with Lauder tomorrow night. You're going to kick all caution to the wind. And you're going to let. It. Happen."

Another muffled *but*.

Hannah's voice went from soft and sweet, to gruff and deep. "Let. It. Happen."

Willow jerked. *"Umph."* Then she nodded, because that was all she could do.

Twenty-four hours later, Willow stood in front of the full-length door mirror in her bedroom. Why in the heck was she so obsessed with her appearance for her date with Lauder? It wasn't like she wanted to impress or entice him. And she definitely had no intentions of *letting it happen*. Regardless of what she'd agreed to under duress.

The elusive *it* made her think of the horror movie with the clown. What if tonight was just as terrifying? What had she gotten herself into? An evening with Lauder. Well, at least in a restaurant full of people, they wouldn't be alone. That was a saving grace.

Why was she putting herself through this torture? Instead of jumping through hoops with Lauder, she could just let Reggie knock her up and forget about all of this fake lover business. No, she couldn't imagine being tied to any man for the next eighteen-plus years. And if what Hannah suspected about Reggie—that he'd fallen for her—was true, he would surely want to stick around and be in the child's life.

Not that Reggie was still an option anyway. She'd severed ties with him. Well, actually, not officially, but she'd declined his company for the past few weeks. She refused to acknowledge Lauder as the reason. He wasn't. Then she recalled the last time she'd been intimate with Reggie. Well, attempted to be intimate. In her head, she couldn't stop seeing Lauder's face. It had ruined the mood. She hadn't seen Reggie since.

The doorbell rang, startling her. *Six o'clock on the dot.* Lauder was punctual. Scrutinizing herself in the mirror once more, she headed out of the bedroom. Opening the door, she eyed the suited stranger standing there. "May I help you?"

"Ms. Dawson?"

"Yes."

"I'm Donovan. Mr. Tolson sent me."

Confused, Willow said, "He sent you?"

"Yes, ma'am. I'm your driver for the evening."

"My driver?"

"Yes, ma'am."

Willow looked past Donovan and spied the black luxury vehicle. No sign of Lauder. "Where is Mr. Tolson?"

"At his residence. I'm to take you there."

"His residence?"

Donovan didn't bother responding this time.

A hundred questions raced through Willow's head. Why had Lauder sent a stranger in a hundred-thousand-dollar vehicle to get her? Why were they going to his residence and not a restaurant? *Where there would be other people*, she added. Was she overdressed?

She ran a hand over the black off-the-shoulder scalloped lace dress that fell just below the knees. *I should change.* A second later, she cast out the idea. Too much energy had been spent on perfecting this look.

"Shall we go?" Donovan asked.

Willow nodded.

Less than a half hour later, she stood face-to-face with

Lauder. Two things she'd learned about him: he was one dynamic kisser, and he could wear the hell out of anything he slid his muscled body into. The dark denim jeans and white button-down shirt were no exceptions.

Again, the top button of his shirt was unfastened, flashing her a scant glimpse of his chest. Her eyes fixed on his Adam's apple, forcing her to swallow hard when her throat suddenly went dry.

When her assessing gaze made an unhurried climb, she flinched at the quizzical expression on Lauder's face. "Um…you don't like wearing ties." Of all the things she could have said, she'd said something so stupid.

"Only when I have to." One corner of his mouth lifted into a sexy smile. "But I can put one on if you prefer."

"You're fine. The tie," she said quickly. "It's…fine." What the hell was wrong with her? Why did Lauder turn her into a blushing fool? *Note to self, you will remain in control tonight.* He flashed that lopsided smile, and her pulse quickened. *Complete control.*

"You look…nice," Lauder said, his eyes roaming over her body.

Nice? A *nice* was all she got? Not wanting to be ungrateful for the mild compliment, she said, "Thank you. So do you. Even without the tie."

"Follow me."

Willow trailed him. For the first time, she really scrutinized the space. He truly did have an amazing home. Decorated in rich stone and a blue-gray color palette with a splash of cream, it suited him. Intense.

The spacious dwelling needed something. But what? It hit her. *Warmth.* It needed warmth, because while it was intense, it was also cold. In that moment, and for some unexplainable reason, she felt empathy for Lauder.

Entering the modern-style kitchen fashioned with all

stainless steel appliances, fixtures and accents, Willow noticed the prep-station-type setup.

"Can you cook?" Lauder asked.

"Umm...*why*?"

"I thought we'd prepare the meal together. But if you'd prefer to go out..."

"No. This is fine."

"You sure? I don't want you to think I'm trying to be cheap."

Willow slid her gaze over the impressive spread atop the marble island: lobster, rib eye steaks, chicken kabobs and an assortment of fresh-cut veggies. Cheap was the last thing floating around in her head. "I'm sure." Cocking a brow, she said, "You can cook?"

"Don't look so surprised. I can burn a kitchen down. Which is exactly what happened during my first cooking lesson."

Willow burst into laughter. "You set a kitchen on fire?"

"It wasn't like a four-alarm fire or anything." He shrugged. "A one-and-a-half alarm, at best."

More laughter poured from Willow.

"Thanks to my foster brother's wife and her bachelors-in-the-kitchen culinary package, I can throw down."

"*You* took cooking lessons?"

Lauder flashed a comical expression. *"Yes."*

"You must have been trying to impress a woman." Lauder's bright expression dimmed, and she couldn't help but wonder why.

"Nah. Most women I come across prefer visiting high-dollar restaurants."

"Not me." God, why had she sounded so desperate? "I mean... I love to tinker in the kitchen, try new things. I watch *a lot* of the cooking channel. I have no life."

Dammit. Why had she admitted that? Admitted any of

that. For one, it sounded as if she were vying for some of his time. For two, she'd made herself sound like a freaking couch potato. For three, she just sounded pitiful.

"Huh" was all Lauder said.

Huh? What did that mean?

Lauder stared at her, narrow eyed, for a moment, then said, "Let's cook."

"Uh, normally, I'd be all for this, but I don't think I have on the proper attire."

"Take it off."

Willow rested a hand on her hip. "You would like that, wouldn't you?"

"What kind of man do you think I am? I'll give you something else to wear." His eyes raked over her. "Mainly because that dress is distracting as hell. I don't want to burn down my kitchen."

Willow lowered her head to hide her smile. Had a man ever alluded to her looking *too* good in a dress? *Nope.* Latching on to his gaze again, she said, "Well, you probably should have mentioned we were going to put your culinary skills to work. I would have worn something less—"

"Sexy?"

"I was going to say fancy."

"Well, I was close enough. Follow me."

A wave of unbridled desire surged through Willow when they entered Lauder's bedroom. While the room they'd just left lacked warmth, this room was hot. Scorching. The burgundy-and-black color scheme bled sensuality. Accents of silver were sprinkled about the room. Possibly to tame the feral space.

Willow's neck, then cheeks, warmed when she eyed the king-size bed. A vision of her and Lauder tangled in the covers burned into her head. Scattering the arousing images, she glanced toward Lauder and realized he'd been watching her.

"I'm sorry, did you say something?" she asked.

"I said you can try it out if you like. It's like sleeping on a cloud."

"So you can tell everyone you had me in your bed again?" She regretted the words as soon as they'd escaped. A second later, she chastised herself for still holding on to the past. It was time to let it go. Lauder had been a stupid teenage boy who'd done a stupid teenage boy thing.

Plus, her exact issue with Lauder hadn't been him telling his boys he'd taken her virginity. It ran much deeper than that. And after all of these years, the pain still lingered. Which was why being here with him was a mistake. All of this was a mistake.

"I have to go, Lauder. I can't do this."

Lauder's jaw clenched. "Don't you move one damn step."

His tone was raspy and commanding. Willow wasn't sure if it was fear or shock that kept her rooted to the floor. When he closed the distance between them and stood dangerously close to her, she experienced a bout of nervous tension.

"You're going to listen to me, Willow. And this time, you're going to hear me."

Ignoring her first instinct—to storm away—she stayed put, curious as to what Lauder had to say to her. But as an act of defiance, she folded her arms across her chest and looked away.

"For years you've believed that I betrayed your trust. Back then, I told you a thousand times I did not tell a single soul about our night together. I wouldn't have, Willow. It was something sacred between the two of us. I wouldn't have cheapened that."

Her gaze slid to him. She had to admit, he sounded just as sincere now as he had the night he'd begged her to believe him. She'd called him a liar and had refused to speak to him from that day forward.

Unable to bear their connection, she looked away again. She wanted to maintain control, had to maintain control. But when she blinked, a tear slid from her eye and down her cheek.

Lauder cradled her face in his hands and guided her to face him. "There's something more going on here. What aren't you telling me?" He dragged his thumb across her cheek. "Talk to me, Willow. I deserve that much."

For some reason, his words touched a nerve. He deserved nothing from her. Yanking away from him, she stormed toward the bedroom door.

"Please, Willow."

The raw emotion in Lauder's voice stopped her.

"Please," he repeated.

This time, something more lingered in his voice. Vulnerability. Pulling in a deep breath, she faced him. "You left me."

Fine lines crawled across his forehead. "Left you?"

"Yes!" Unshed tears stung her eyes. "I was angry at you when I thought you'd told all your boys you'd taken my virginity, and I would have eventually forgiven you. But what hurt, what truly hurt, was you fighting Bad Breath Marvin just to be moved to another group home." Her voice cracked. "Just to get away from me. You got what you wanted, then you left me alone in that hellhole. You were the only friend I had, Lauder. You were the closest thing to love I'd ever known." Tears streamed down her face. "You left me to—" She stopped shy of saying *handle the miscarriage alone*. He'd had no idea she'd been carrying his child. Neither had she until it was too late. But had he been there… "You left me," she repeated. "And you broke my heart."

Lauder ran a hand back and forth over his head. His face contorted, relaxed, then contorted again. "Is that—" His words caught, and he briefly glanced away. A second or two later, he returned his attention to her. "You thought I *intentionally* got myself sent to The Cardinal House to get away from you?"

It was what she'd been told by several of the other girls at their group home. And at sixteen, she'd believed it. "Yes," she mumbled.

Lauder looked as if he'd been punched in the chest. The strong, confident man she encountered every time they were together was now gone, replaced with a man who seemed unsure and confused.

He shook his head. "That's the furthest thing from the truth." Closing the distance between them again, he said, "I'd found out Marvin was the one who'd told everyone about us."

"Marvin?" she said absently.

He nodded. "The pervert had followed us into the woods and watched. *That's* why I kicked his ass."

Willow vividly remembered that fight. It'd sounded like a bomb had gone off in the recreation room. Once she'd broken through the crowd of gawkers, she'd been stunned to see Lauder straddling Marvin, his strong hands wrapped around Marvin's neck. It'd taken several of the other boys to pull Lauder off him.

"I told Marvin I planned to kick his ass for every person he'd told. He went to Head Lady and told her I'd threatened him. That's why I was sent away. Not to get away from you. I didn't want to leave. I didn't have a choice. But I couldn't tell you any of this because you weren't speaking to me, remember?"

Willow didn't know what to say. This was all so much to take in. She'd gotten it wrong. She'd gotten it so wrong. Finally finding her voice, she said, "I—I didn't know."

Lauder's tone was firm when he spoke. "Of course you didn't. You were too busy being stubborn as hell. Too busy *still* being stubborn as hell."

Willow lowered her head. She'd hated him all these years because she thought he'd abandoned her. All the while, he'd been protecting her honor. She'd lugged this hurt and pain around like a travel chest, avoiding relationships because she'd never wanted to feel that kind of heartache again.

Meeting his gaze, she said the first thing that came to mind, "I'm sorry." And hoped it was enough.

Chapter 6

Lauder felt responsible for every tear Willow had shed. Now and years ago. At least now he understood her animosity against him. It tore him up inside that for so long, she'd believed he'd been running from her. Hadn't she known how he'd felt about her back then?

Obviously not.

This wasn't how he'd imagined their night going, but he was glad the truth had come out. Now, they could move on. Together, if he had his way. But he wouldn't rush things. He'd take his time winning her over.

"I'll forgive you, Willow. Under one condition."

An unsure expression spread over her face. "What's the condition?"

"That you forgive me, also."

Willow's brow furrowed. "Forgive you? What's there to forgive?"

"I should have made you listen to me back then, instead of accepting your silent treatment."

Willow flashed a half smile. "As if you could have *made* me listen. I'm stubborn as hell, remember?"

Lauder laughed. Sobering, he said, "I have an idea. Let's hug it out."

"What?"

"Let's hug it out. Hug away the past. Get rid of all the bad blood between us. We still have to work together, remember? We really shouldn't have any tension between us."

It would have been a lie had he said *getting rid of bad blood* was the only reason he wanted to wrap his arms around Willow. Ever since the day she'd kissed him in his office, he'd longed to feel her warm body pressed against his again. Yes, it would be torture to hold her and not be able to do anything else, but it would be worth it.

If he were a mouse in a maze chasing her thoughts, he was sure he'd be drop-dead tired. Anxious, he waited as Willow clearly grappled with the suggestion. He couldn't remember the last time his heart thundered so furiously in his chest. It was sad, really, how overly eager he was to feel her in his arms. But everyone had a weakness. Willow was becoming his.

Actually, he could remember a time he'd been even more anxious than now. It was the night he'd kissed her slowly, lowered her onto the patch of cotton-soft grass and promised her he'd be gentle. It had been her first time. And unbeknownst to Willow, it had been his first time, too. To date, it was still the best day of his life.

As ridiculous as it sounded, no other lover he'd had in his bed had come close to making him feel the way Willow had made him feel that day. Something had happened to him that warm July evening: he'd fallen in love with Willow. And at seventeen, he'd been convinced he and Willow would always be together. Unfortunately, real life had snatched them apart.

Willow's gentle words drew him back to present time. Some vibrancy had returned to her beautiful eyes, and he took it as a good sign.

"You don't hate me? For casting you as a villain all of these years?" she asked.

"I could never hate you, Willow. Ever."

The corners of her mouth quirked into a smile. "Good." She shrugged. "So, are we doing this? *Hugging it out.*"

"Come here, woman."

Not allowing another minute to snake past without having Willow in his arms, Lauder took the initiative and secured her in a close, body-warming embrace. Hesitation lingered in Willow's limbs loosely touching him. But several moments later, her hold tightened.

Lauder hummed, "Mmm. I can feel the bad blood flowing out already." That wasn't the only place blood flowed.

"I can feel it, too. It feels so good."

Willow's tone was silky, sensual. Lauder slowly reared back, his mouth so close to hers he could feel the warm breath on his cheek from her partially opened mouth. He wanted to kiss her, and by the glint in her tender eyes, she would have allowed him.

Yes, he desperately wanted her lips against his. So badly he could taste them. But he wanted something else even more. For her to trust him. As difficult as it was, he fought the impulse to ravish her tempting mouth. They'd made progress. He didn't want to be responsible for any setback.

Selfishly, he wanted Willow to crave him, too. Crave him so intensely that he was the only thing she thought about when she fell asleep at night, and the first image to burn into her head when she woke.

Lauder reluctantly released her. "We better get dinner started. I'm starving." However, food wasn't what he hungered for. His greedy desire was for Willow's body. Every inch of it. The things he wanted to do to her right now... Sinful things. Erotic things. Things that would make her body bend in ways she'd never experienced. He was no longer the inexperienced seventeen-year-old boy who'd somehow managed to bring her to an orgasm; he was a man who knew his way around the female form.

"So am I," she said. "Starving." As if she'd realized how sultry her words had been, she jerked, then took a step back. "I'll take that change of clothes."

Lauder grinned when Willow's cheeks turned a rosy color. Providing her with a T-shirt with his company's logo across the front and a pair of black gym pants, he left her alone in his bedroom.

Several minutes later, Willow made her way into the kitchen. "Well, I won't win any awards for stellar fashion, but I'm really comfortable."

Even in the oversize attire, Lauder found her insanely attractive. His eyes lowered to her bare feet, her nails painted with polish that sparkled under the lighting. Even her feet were sexy. When she burst out laughing, his gaze met hers.

"Really?" She pointed to his chest.

Lauder lowered his eyes to the front of the apron he wore. "What?"

"'Warning: delicious dark chocolate,'" Willow read.

He shrugged. "I've been told I should come with a warning label. So... I got one."

Willow laughed again as if it were the funniest thing she'd ever heard. Lauder pulled a hand to his waist, trying not to let her amusement clip away at his ego. "Okay, okay. It wasn't that funny."

She flashed a palm. "I'm sorry." Another snicker slipped out. "Sorry."

"Ha, ha. Yours is over there." He'd had it specially printed just for her. Unsure whether the image still held significance, he waited for her reaction.

Willow unfolded the black fabric, her mouth falling

open. "A dragonfly." She smiled, running a finger over the white fancy letters spelling out her name.

"I wasn't sure if dragonflies were still your thing."

"They are." She slipped her head in the loop, then turned. "Will you tie me?"

Yes, he would. To the bed. To a chair. Curtailing his X-rated thoughts, he said, "Sure." Unhurried, he fiddled with the apron strings. His eyes drifted to her backside, inches from his front side. When he imagined bending her over one of the bar stools and burying himself deep inside her, his shaft twitched in his pants and started to swell.

"I'm surprised you remembered."

The sound of Willow's voice snatched his thoughts away from making wild, hot, passionate love to her. *In due time*, he told himself. "Are you kidding? You had dragonfly everything: notebooks, stickers, charms." He chuckled. "I never understood why you were so fascinated with them. Butterflies, I could see. But dragonflies..."

Willow turned and sadness shadowed her previous lively mood. Had he said something wrong?

"I was left inside a church when I was three. There was a note pinned to my dress: *Please take care of my little dragonfly, because I no longer can.* I also held a stuffed brown bear, a green dragonfly stitched at its stomach."

Shit. Now he felt like a total ass for devaluing the dragonfly. "Willow... I'm sorry. I didn't—"

Willow snickered, then slapped her hand over her mouth. A beat later, she burst into laughter. "For a politician, you sure are gullible."

Lauder brought his hands to his waist and crooked a brow. "Wait. You made all of that up?"

Willow pursed her lips and nodded.

"Oh, that was wrong," he said, inching toward her.

"And you need to pay for messing with my emotions like that."

Willow backed away, but before she could make a grand escape, he scooped her into his arms. She squirmed and laughed so hard that tears ran from the corners of her eyes. This was how he liked seeing her, elated. What was even better, he was the cause of her mirth.

"I'm not sure what I'm going to do with you, woman, but it's not going to be pretty," he said.

"Okay, okay. I'll tell you the real reason. Just put me down," she said through laughter. "I'm going to pee on myself." Her eyes widened, then she laughed more. "I can't believe I just said that."

Lauder placed her back on her feet. "Bathroom's down the hall on the right."

She took a step in that direction, but stopped and turned to face him again. "I wasn't very popular in school… Well, you know that already. My hair wasn't as long as the other girls', my skin not as light. I was flat chested and had no butt." She laughed gently, then massaged the crook of her neck. "Anyway. Mrs. Sutherland— our middle school history teacher—pulled me aside one day and gave me a dragonfly pendant. When she presented it to me, she'd said, 'Everything has beauty, but not everyone sees it.'"

"Confucius."

Willow nodded. "I like butterflies, Lauder, but I relate more to the dragonfly and its unseen beauty."

He leaned a hip against the counter and folded his arms across his chest. "You're breathtaking, Willow. Then and now."

Willow mimicked his stance. Grinning, she said, "If I recall correctly, Lauder Tolson, you were one of my tormentors. You never missed an opportunity to pull my hair or call me Weeping Willow."

Instantly, Lauder regretted taunting Willow when they were young. While he didn't recall anything else he'd done to tease her, he did remember pulling her hair and making fun of her name. However, his motivation had been that of an immature child, nothing malicious. He'd liked her. It wasn't until he was older that he'd learned there was a more effective way of expressing that.

"Because I liked you," he admitted. "I wanted to make sure you noticed me." He laughed. "It took you several years, but you finally did."

"I always knew you were there, Lauder. I was just never sure of your motives."

"They were always honorable, I swear."

Willow repositioned herself, her backside now against the counter, and lowered her gaze to her fiddling fingers. "Lauder, our night together…" She paused and took a deep breath. "We, um… I got…"

"We shared something beautiful."

Willow's head slowly turned toward him, and she smiled. "Yeah, we did."

She stared into his eyes, apparently searching. But what was she looking for? Possibly for a sign that he truly meant what he'd said about their first time together. His eyes skimmed every inch of her face. She identified with a dragonfly's unseen beauty. Really? This woman had to know just how damn beautiful she was. Those sparkling, brilliant eyes. That cute button nose. And those lips.

His gaze fixed on her mouth. His stomach knotted and tightened more and more with every second he tortured himself with the memory of those cloud-soft lips against his. Jerking away from the tangle of temptation, he slid his gaze away.

"Um, let's start dinner. We should—" Lauder stopped, pressed his palms into the cold marble, leaned his weight into his arms and lowered his head. What the hell was he doing? When had he ever denied himself something he wanted? Especially something—or someone—as much as he wanted Willow.

Willow rested her hand on his arm, then snatched it away. "What's wrong?"

Hell if he knew. The only thing he knew for sure was it only occurred when they were together. He wanted to casually label it lust or longing, but he couldn't lie to himself; it was much more than a need to bed Willow. She was doing something to him, something internally, and he was powerless to stop it.

Eyeing Willow, he could see he wasn't the only one struggling with whatever was happening between them.

Chapter 7

Willow's heart thudded in her chest, and her lips tingled to be touched by Lauder's. A good tingle. A tingle that matched the one between her legs. Lauder's probing gaze searched her eyes. There was no use trying to hide her longing. She was sure her face gave everything away. Now, all she needed was for him to lead. She'd definitely follow.

So, why wasn't he kissing her?

By the look in his dark, hungry eyes, he desperately wanted to. What was holding him back? Maybe her face wasn't as revealing as she thought.

Could she be misreading him? No. That was pure desire swimming in his eyes. He wanted her, and she wanted him, too.

Wanted him to kiss her.

Wanted him to touch her.

Wanted him, period.

Willow desperately wanted Lauder to dip forward and capture her mouth. Kiss her slow, gentle. Take his time exploring every inch of it with his skillful tongue. Inwardly, she moaned with deep satisfaction. Outwardly, she waited for him to make a move.

Her taut nipples beaded tight in her bra. Warm sensations swirled in her stomach. Her clit pounded, desperate for Lauder's delicate touch.

Wetness pooled between her legs, her body's way of letting her know just how much she wanted—no, needed—this. Deliriously impatient, she fought against screaming "Just kiss me already" at the top of her lungs. But she chose to preserve what little control she still held.

Her legs wobbled with fantasies of Lauder's large hands combing over her, claiming her as his—even if it was only for a night.

One night?

The thought taunted her when she considered the frenzy her body was in. What if one night wasn't enough? No man had ever awakened her body this way. And with just a heated look. Well, she couldn't really call this deliciously paralyzing thing Lauder was doing to her just a look. She'd been *just* looked at before. This was a thorough declaration of intent.

So why wasn't he acting on it?

Kiss me. Kiss me, please.

Why wasn't she bold enough to ask for exactly what she wanted? Or maybe she was. But before she could act on impulse, fate intervened, possibly saving her from herself.

Ding-dong.

Willow asked herself whether or not the doorbell had actually sounded, when Lauder didn't respond to the chime. Had he not heard it? Had she really heard it? She broke their trancelike connection when it rang again, providing confirmation. Lauder pinched his brows together, causing lines to crawl between them.

"What's wrong?" he asked.

Willow chuckled. "There's someone at the door."

"How do you know?"

Just then, the doorbell chimed again. She flashed him a *that's how* look. She liked the idea of him being so into her that he'd been too disoriented to hear his own doorbell.

Lauder cursed under his breath. "I forgot Chuck, my campaign manager—" he clarified "—said he might swing by. I didn't actually think he would."

Lauder sounded disappointed by the intrusion. However, she was relieved. Maybe the interruption had been for the best. What if they had kissed, or gone even further and slept together? Reminding herself that she had one goal here and one goal only—to adopt a child, not get romantically involved with a politician—might help to refocus her.

She could vaguely hear the conversation Lauder was having with Chuck. A second later, Chuck strolled into the room, followed by a distressed-looking Lauder. Lauder mouthed the word "Sorry."

"It's okay," she mouthed back.

Willow studied Chuck. Hannah would love him. Tall, dark, incredibly handsome. And he wore the heck out of a tailored suit. He also wore the heck out of something else—a scowl. The man was too darn attractive to look so grouchy.

Chuck's appraising dark eyes raked over her borrowed attire, probably silently questioning her fashion choices. As if mechanical, his arm jutted out toward her. The move was so sudden, she flinched.

"Willow, I presume."

The man never cracked a smile. Willow took his hand. "Yes." His firm grip screamed confidence. Made sense. "Nice to meet you."

"Chuck Carlisle. Lauder's campaign manager. Nice to meet you, too. Heard a lot about you."

"Nice things, I hope."

"Of course," Chuck said, tossing a glance in Lauder's direction.

"Well, I should go. Give you two some privacy," Willow said.

"No," Lauder said, almost too quickly.

"He's right. You should stay," Chuck said. "We need to make sure we're all on the same page, and that there are no surprises."

The way Chuck eyed her, it almost felt like he was accusing her of hiding something.

Willow followed Lauder and Chuck into the living room and eased down into the chair. Lauder sat beside her. He leaned forward, resting his forearms on his thighs, and interlocked his fingers in front of him. His left leg bounced against the hardwood. What had him so anxious?

Chuck spent the next hour giving her a code of conduct of sorts. In a nutshell, the dos: keep responses to the media short and sweet, be an adoring couple, always assume someone is watching; the don'ts: don't share this arrangement with anyone and don't screw up.

Well, she'd already broken one of the don'ts by telling Hannah.

Chuck fished inside his briefcase. "Now that we've covered the logistics," he said, passing her a short stack of papers, "if you could read and sign this nondisclosure agreement."

Lauder lowered his head as if the request saddened him. His bouncing leg increased in speed. Was this the source of his unease?

The fact that he refused to even glance in her direction led her to believe this was all Chuck's idea. Or was it?

Scanning the papers, she said, "I'm guessing that having my attorney review this is out of the question."

"The fewer people who know about this, the better," Chuck said. "It's standard lingo. There's nothing—"

"Pen." Something told her Lauder wouldn't put her in harm's way or allow Chuck to, either.

When Chuck offered her an expensive-looking piece, she scribbled her name, then passed it and the papers back to him.

"Thank you," Lauder said, finally breaking his silence.

"Yes, thank you," Chuck said, storing them both inside his briefcase and turning his attention to Lauder.

For what felt like an eternity, Chuck filled Lauder in on how they would be focusing on the women's vote for the next few weeks, a Meet the Media event and several other upcoming appearances, including a visit to the Wake County Senior Women for Change organization.

"I can read your mind, L," Chuck said, "but you're just going to have to trust me on this. These senior ladies could catapult you to the top and right out of Edmondson's reach. This demographic of women aren't feeling Edmondson, but they are unsure about you. You're 'inexperienced' and that scares them. They need to know you can get shit done." He slid his gaze to Willow. "Pardon my French."

Willow nodded.

Chuck continued, "You already have the younger female vote. Mainly because most of them want to sleep with you."

At Chuck's claim, Willow felt a twinge of jealousy until she recalled the fact that Lauder didn't belong to her. He was free to sleep with whom he pleased. But she'd be the first to admit that the thought bothered her. Far more than it should have, given their true relationship status.

"Do you want to sleep with me?" Lauder whispered, bumping her playfully.

Her cheeks burned with embarrassment, because while Chuck didn't glance up from his folder, she was 110 percent sure he'd heard Lauder.

Chuck continued, "But the older female vote is still up for grabs by either party. Your talking points on social security, Medicare and the other senior-related issues are solid, but it's going to take more than smooth talk to win those votes. Like I said, they're unsure about you. You're going to have to charm the hell out of these women."

"Charming won't work," Willow had said before she knew it.

Chuck's sharp eyes darted toward her. After studying her a second or two, he said, "Why not?"

"These are seasoned women." She eyed Lauder. "Yes, your charisma might work on all those young women wanting so eagerly to sleep with you, but these women aren't easily wooed by a handsome face and mesmerizing smile."

Lauder grinned. "You think my smile is mesmerizing?"

Willow jostled him playfully. "Can you focus, please?"

Lauder pouted. "Sorry."

"These are mothers, grandmothers, great-grandmothers. Plus, they've lived in times when things weren't so easy for women. They were forced to wear a smile and hide their suffering. Just like us."

Lauder looked away from her and studied his intertwined fingers.

"If you want to reach them, you're going to have to be more personal, relatable. Talk about your past. That'll get their attention. That'll get their votes."

"Huh," Chuck said, leaning back against the plush cushions.

After a long while, Lauder spoke, directing his abrupt words at her. "How often do you talk about your past?"

"I don't," she said. "Ever."

"But you want me to relive mine?" Lauder pushed to his feet, ambled to the floor-to-ceiling window and stared out. A second later, he shoved his hands into his pockets.

As close as they had been back then, he hadn't shared much of his past with her. Willow, of all people, understood his reluctance to bare his soul to a room filled with strangers. Sometimes memories were more painful than events.

"Will you be there?" Lauder asked to no one in particular.

"Of course I'll be there," Chuck said.

Lauder turned. "Not you." He eyed Willow.

Willow didn't understand why Lauder would ask the question. She'd agreed to play a role and intended to do it to the best of her ability. Maybe he thought that after their heated exchange in the kitchen she'd changed her mind. After such an intense moment, she probably should have. "In the front row," she said without hesitation.

Though Lauder flashed a lazy smile, Willow could tell something still bothered him. All that came to mind was something from his past. She briefly thought about her own past. While she'd joshed Lauder about being abandoned in a church at three, it hadn't been that far from the truth. She hadn't been three, she'd been four. It hadn't been a church, it had been a filthy truck stop bathroom.

The only part of the story that had been accurate was the note, but not 100 percent accurate. It hadn't said *Take care of my dragonfly*. It had read *Take care of my most precious gift because I cannot*.

Most precious gift.

Who sacrificed their most precious gift?

The sound of Chuck's voice pulled her from her thoughts. "I'm sorry. What did you say?"

"I asked about Reggie Spivey."

Willow's body tensed, and she was sure both men had seen it. Her gaze slid urgently to Lauder, then away. "A friend." She massaged the space between her neck and shoulder. "He's just a friend."

Without glancing in Lauder's direction again, she could feel his accusing eyes burning a hole into her. Daring to look at him, she winced from the hard expression on his face. Was he angry at the mention of Reggie? Jealous? He had no right to be either.

Lauder shifted back toward the window, mimicking his earlier pose. Only this time, he crossed his arms over his chest and rolled his head on his shoulders as if to relieve tension.

Willow turned toward Chuck, her brow furrowed. "How do you know about Reggie?" It was a legitimate question. The only way he could have known was if he'd…investigated her. The thought made the blood boil in her veins. She'd agreed to be a part of this ruse; she hadn't agreed to be placed under the microscope.

Chuck eyed her like a vulture just waiting for her to keel over so he could pick her bones clean. "It's my job to know. It's also my job to make sure Lauder is protected at all times. So if there's—"

"Chuck," Lauder said, not bothering to face them.

Willow flinched at the bass present in Lauder's voice. His warning was stern, protective. Had she not wanted to claw Chuck's eyes out, she probably would have appreciated it more.

Chuck sighed heavily and stood. "We'll talk later, L." He eyed Willow. "No disrespect. I'm just doing my job."

If she tilted her head just right, what he flashed could have possibly been considered a smile, but it didn't last long enough for her to truly analyze it. Wow. Had she ever met anyone as…focused, she settled on for lack of a better word, as Chuck?

But while he displayed a hard outer shell, his eyes suggested he wasn't as tough as he pretended to be. Something told her he needed a Hannah in his life. That woman could draw out the best in anyone.

"Night, folks."

Willow stood when Lauder finally turned away from the window.

He buzzed right past her. "I'll grab your dress and drive you home."

Apparently, she had read him accurately. He was angry, or jealous, or both. But why? They weren't an item. They were two people perpetrating a fraud. *Fake lovers.*

"Okay," Willow mumbled to herself, because Lauder had escaped from the room.

Several minutes later, they were inside Lauder's sleek all-black Mustang Shelby GT. The muscle car was as sexy as he was. Though she never would have guessed he'd own a car such as this. When he started the engine, it made a sound that demanded attention. On second thought, the car suited him.

Out of the hotel parking lot, Lauder made a right onto Wilmington Street, then another right onto Martin. He handled the vehicle with precision and care.

"Are you comfortable?" he asked. "I can adjust the temp."

Still the gentleman. "I'm fine. This is a beautiful vehicle."

"Thanks. I got her last month. A birthday present to myself."

"March 17…"

Lauder's head reared back. "You remember."

"I do."

A beat of silence played between them.

"Her?"

He chuckled. "Something this sexy has to be a woman, right?"

"I guess."

At least he seemed to be warming up to her again. Too bad she was about to cool things down now. Despite feeling like she didn't owe him an explanation, this had to be said. "I wasn't completely honest with Chuck. About Reggie."

"I gathered as much. You do this thing to your shoulder when you're not being truthful."

Dammit. She had to be more careful.

"So…you two are in a relationship?"

It was more of a comment than a question.

"Not exactly," she said, setting her eyes straight ahead.

"Ah. Friends with benefits."

She didn't confirm, nor deny, the claim. Out of her peripheral vision, she saw Lauder's hand tighten on the steering wheel.

"Are you two still involved?"

"No. Not since…" Her words trailed. She couldn't tell him she'd lost all interest in Reggie when he'd stepped on the scene. That was giving him too much power over her. "No," she repeated, facing him.

Lauder's eyes lowered to her mouth, and a twinge of desire sparked through her. She extinguished the flick before it became a flame.

"About what almost happened back at my place… Between us," he clarified.

She didn't bother asking him to elaborate, because she knew exactly what he was referring to. The moment they'd both nearly succumbed to passion. "What about it?"

"It can't happen."

Clearly, he'd experienced a moment of clarity, too. "I know," she said, regretting ever allowing herself to want him.

Chapter 8

Willow loved the feel of the bubbles tickling her feet and was glad she'd let Hannah talk her into coming for a mani-pedi. Particularly on a Sunday. Sundays for her were usually reserved for the Lord and unwinding from a long week. But after the evening she'd had with Lauder the night before, she needed this moment of relaxation.

She closed her eyes and allowed her head to fall back against the plush burgundy leather massaging pedicure chair. If she kept them closed too long, she might just fall asleep. She hadn't slept much at all the night before. Most of the night had been spent trying to assure herself that she could go through with this charade with Lauder.

Hannah's voice filtered into Willow's head.

"And he didn't give any explanation at all?" Hannah asked.

"No. And I didn't ask for one. I just agreed with him that it couldn't happen, because it can't." Her head rose. "I feel like such a fool for even thinking of crossing that line with Lauder." A humorless laugh escaped. "I would have felt like even a bigger fool had we slept together and this morning he'd said that to me. I guess I should be thankful for small favors and interruptions."

"You shouldn't feel like a fool. If anyone should feel foolish, it's him. Going all bipolar on you."

Willow absently fingered the champagne glass of orange juice she'd been given. "It was the strangest thing, Hannah. One minute, things were super-duper hot and tempting. The next, he's pretty much kicking me out of his place. He completely shut down on me."

"I'm telling you, it's because of Reggie. Men are like that. Like territorial animals. He didn't like the idea of another man rolling around in the sheets with his woman." Hannah leaned forward in laughter.

Willow swatted at her playfully. "I'm not his woman." She bit at the corner of her lip. Hearing about Reggie seemed like the most logical explanation for Lauder's shift, but something told her that wasn't it. At least, not wholly. "The more I think about it, I'm glad nothing happened between us. Nothing good could have come out of it. Everything we share is based on a lie. I have a job to do. I shouldn't have allowed my raging libido to cloud my common sense. I have a job to do," she repeated, this time with less enthusiasm. "And when it's done, I'm going to kiss Lauder Tolson goodbye."

At the mention of kissing Lauder, Willow replayed the one time they had kissed in his office and took a sip from her glass to cool down her rising core temp.

Hannah fanned Willow with her hand. "Shake his hand instead. I'm not sure you can handle kissing him again." She barked another laugh.

"I hate you so much right now," Willow said with laughter in her tone.

Silence played between them a moment.

"You know, Will, something good has already come from your reconnecting with Lauder."

Willow eyed Hannah with genuine confusion, unable

to think of one single good thing that had come out of any of this. Let's see, she'd destroyed a perfectly good block of clay. She'd sold her soul to the devil. She'd almost made a complete fool of herself. She'd lost valuable sleep. The list could go on and on.

Nope. Nothing good.

But for kicks, she said, "What, exactly?"

"You learned the truth about the man you'd loved as a young girl. Found out he hadn't betrayed you, hadn't abandoned you. You've been freed from the weight of all that past baggage."

Okay, maybe there was one good thing. She did feel lighter. But something still weighed her down. The miscarriage. She still hadn't shared it with Lauder, but she'd tried to last night. Heck, maybe she shouldn't tell him. It was a long time ago. Did it even matter now? After all this time? *What would be the point?* Her heart had bled enough for the both of them over losing their child. A child she hadn't even known she'd been carrying until she'd suffered horrible cramping and bleeding and had to be rushed to the hospital.

No, she'd spare Lauder that burden.

"You could walk away from all of this, you know?" Hannah's words were cautious.

She'd considered that, but that was probably what Lauder was expecting her to do. No, she would see this thing through. "We have a binding agreement." And there was a signed contract to prove it.

"Like he would sue you and expose himself."

"He wouldn't, but that pit bull of a campaign manager would." And would probably twist the facts so severely she'd definitely be found guilty and sentenced to life imprisonment.

"Do you still have feelings for him?"

Willow faced Hannah with urgency. "No." She massaged the side of her neck. "It's been almost two decades. Still caring about him after all of that time would be ridiculous. Foolish."

Hannah flashed sympathetic eyes. "Will, I'm the last person you need to hide from. He was your first love. He'll always be in your heart. He was your first lover. He'll always have a part of you that no other man can *ever* claim."

Willow slid her gaze away and swallowed the painful lump rising in the back of her throat. Maybe seeing Lauder again had sparked…*something*. Something that was easier to label as lust, but it felt like so much more.

She took a sip from her glass. How would she get through the next several months romping around town with a man whom she found extremely hard to resist? A man she *had* to resist. That *something* she felt had to be contained. She would play the game and be the biggest cheerleader Lauder had.

And when all was said and done, she'd kiss—handshake—Lauder goodbye.

Lauder relaxed in one of the mocha leather sofa chairs inside his office, passing a stress ball back and forth from one hand to the other. Chuck occupied the opposite identical chair, giving Lauder an update on his schedule.

While his mind should have been on the campaign and his upcoming events, it wasn't. His thoughts were on Willow and their date-turned-disaster. Three days, and he was still kicking himself for doing a complete one-eighty on her.

Chuck tossed something on the wooden table that separated them, drawing Lauder from his thoughts. "What's this?"

"A copy of the nondisclosure agreement for Willow's records."

Lauder lifted it and studied her signature on the back page. He felt some way about having her sign the agreement, like he was implying he didn't trust her.

"Did she mention it after I left the other night?" Chuck asked.

Lauder filtered back to their conversation. "No, she didn't mention it." His gaze rose to Chuck. "I do wish you would have given me a heads-up."

"I should have. I apologize for that. I could tell you wanted to protest, but I'm glad you didn't. One of my many jobs is to protect you."

Lauder tossed the papers back on the table. "It's not necessary. You—"

"It is necessary. You might believe—"

"—you were right," Lauder continued, cutting off Chuck's rant. "Willow is a bad idea." He fell back against the cushion. "You can choose someone else. I won't object."

Chuck's expression did a slow morph from stunned to confused, then he laughed. "Come on, L. Don't tell me you're upset because she had something with that Reggie Spivey character. You weren't even in the picture then."

As much as Lauder hated the idea of Reggie Spivey—any man—having his way with Willow, that wasn't it. He hugged one of the decorative pillows to his chest. "I'm too vulnerable around her, Chuck. Weak."

Chuck nodded slowly. "You're definitely different when you're with her, but I wouldn't call it weakness. Less intense, maybe."

Clearly, that was his best friend talking. "I hated her idea of baring my soul at the seniors' event. *Hated* it," he emphasized. "But when she said she'd be there and in the front row... I felt this overwhelming sense of relief. This unexplainable courage."

"O...kay," Chuck said as if he didn't see what the big deal was.

Lauder sat forward with urgency, tossing the pillow aside. "I've never had any woman, *any* woman, affect me like this one. I don't like it."

"Why?"

How did he know that question was coming. *Why?* Lauder shrugged. "I don't know. Maybe the idea of one woman—any woman—having that kind of influence over me scares me a little."

Chuck looked as if he were thoroughly considering Lauder's words. A beat later, he said, "I get it."

Chuck sat forward, resting his elbows on his thighs and absently twisting his wedding band around his finger. He'd lost his wife in an automobile accident two years ago. Lauder felt sympathy for his friend who still wore the piece that brought him both a great deal of strength and a great deal of pain.

Chuck recovered from his moment and sighed heavily. "Well, you're just going to have to suck it up, because it's too late to renege. The wheels are already in motion."

Lauder narrowed his eyes. "What did you do?"

"Leaked a little info to a friend about your budding romance. Plus, as much as it pains me to admit this, I was wrong about Willow. I think she's the perfect one for the part. She has spunk and a backbone."

Lauder cocked a brow. "Who are you, and what have you done with Chuckie?"

Chuck barked a laugh. "I like her. She's not catty like the women you usually associate with."

"Willow and I aren't dating."

Chuck ignored him and continued, "Willow's smart

and thinks fast on her feet. More important, she seems genuinely concerned about seeing you succeed." He stood. "You may not want her, but you got her. At least for the next several months."

That was the problem. He wanted her. More than anything he'd ever wanted in his life.

Chapter 9

"Are you nervous?"

The calm and smooth timbre of Lauder's voice pulled Willow's focus away from the world whizzing by the car window. Shaking her head, she said, "No." It was a lie but not for the reason Lauder was asking.

They were on their way to the senior event where Lauder would stand in front of dozens of mature women and try to convince them he could *get shit done*—as Chuck had so eloquently put it. And she would be in the midst of it all.

But that wasn't what had her uneasy. It was the fact that she sat so close to Lauder in the back of the sleek chauffeured sedan. And he smelled so damn good. Like strength and confidence with a hint of oak. And he looked dazzling. Like he was about to grace a runway in Paris, not stand on a makeshift stage inside the NC State Mc-Kimmon Center.

"Good" was all he said before returning his focus to the notes Chuck had given him.

"Are you?"

"No. Public speaking doesn't bother me."

"Something bothered you," she said before even realizing it was coming. When Lauder leveled a quizzical gaze on her, she continued, "When it was first mentioned back at your place, you seemed...hesitant."

Willow wasn't sure why that moment had stuck with her for the past week. Possibly because whatever the reason, it could have something to do with his shift that night also. Another thing she wasn't sure of...why that night still bothered her. She knew the two of them having a strictly business relationship was for the best; why couldn't her body receive the message? And hadn't she decided to simply focus on their arrangement and be Lauder's biggest cheerleader, nothing else?

Their arrangement.

It sounded so clandestine.

Maybe because that was exactly what it was.

Secret.

Covert.

Concealed.

And countless other synonyms that could be thrown in.

Lauder's jaw clenched. It had been faint but her eyes were trained to see small details others would miss or ignore. His jaw relaxed a second later. What was going on with him? And why was she so invested in finding out the answer?

"Honestly, I originally thought it would be a waste of time. I believed these women would never vote for me. So, the businessman in me thought it best to spend my time and energy in areas guaranteed to produce a return on investment. I had to switch to the politician. Every individual is a potential vote, right?"

His answer made sense, except for the *guaranteed* part. Nothing in life was guaranteed. No matter how well you planned or strategized, something always went wrong. Considering what she and Lauder were doing, the nothing's guaranteed fact should have shaken her credence.

Several minutes later, Willow occupied a chair in the front row and directly in the line of sight of Lauder. These spunky seniors hurled question after question at him, and he'd handled them like a pro. He truly was great in a public setting.

So far, Lauder had skirted by without having to go too deep into his past. She'd been wrong. This charm thing seemed to be working after all.

"We'll take one last question," the moderator said, a tall middle-aged man with wiry brown hair, intense eyes and an even more severe expression.

A petite woman with lilac hair raised a frail-looking hand. When the moderator gave her the go-ahead, she rose to her feet and accepted the handheld mic from the runner.

"Ma'am, please state your name and question."

She cleared her throat as if preparing to bellow a Sunday hymn. "Good afternoon. I'm Carissa Waldron," she said with vigor. "Thank you, Mr. Tolson, for being here today to entertain us old folks and our concerns."

The room filled with laughter. Lauder flashed one of those ridiculously spectacular smiles, and Willow swore Ms. Waldron blushed.

"Happy to be here," Lauder said once the room quieted.

Ms. Waldron continued, "I'm nearing ninety years old."

Willow cocked a brow. With the woman's full face of makeup and trendy pantsuit—that coincidentally matched her hair—she wouldn't have guessed a day over sixty at most.

"I'm a retired schoolteacher living on an extremely fixed income. Like many in this room, some months I had to choose between food and medication. I've gone hungry, been cold, have sat in the dark. I've dealt with a lot, Mr. Tolson. Seen even more. Including politicians making promises they never intend to keep."

Willow slid a glance toward the stage. Lauder eyed Ms. Waldron intently, as if he were hanging to her every word, eager to hear all she had to say. Willow returned her attention to Ms. Waldron.

Ms. Waldron continued, "I'd imagine most politicians have never known hardship, and therefore, don't understand the needs and struggles of the disenfranchised. And of course, after being elected into power, they no longer feel our plight is a worthy enough agenda to continue to pursue. Tell me, young man, how are you any different?"

The question garnered a round of applause. Again, Willow noted the jaw clench she doubted anyone else in the room witnessed. Lauder gripped the sides of the podium and leaned forward slightly. His attention slid from Ms. Waldron and settled directly on Willow.

The intensity of their connection snatched her breath away. They'd eyed one another plenty, but never like this. His gaze seeped past her eyes and peered into her soul. She could feel his turmoil as if she were going through it, too.

For the first time ever, she saw a trace of something in his expression. Not quite fear, but definitely not the cloak of fortitude he usually donned so prominently. The urge to rush to the stage and wrap her arms around him was overwhelming.

But that wouldn't help him. Sometimes, all someone needed was to know that someone had their back. So, she mouthed, "I'm right here." Whether it helped or not, she didn't know, but when Lauder's white-knuckled hold on the wood loosened, she considered it had.

Lauder slid his eyes back to Ms. Waldron. "I've known

plenty of hardship. I do understand, Ms. Waldron. My childhood consisted of being shuffled from one group home to another. One temporary foster family after another."

He moved from behind the comfort and security of the podium, descended the stairs and stood face-to-face with Ms. Waldron. Willow could only imagine how hard this was for Lauder, but his stride, his stance, his expression suggested he was in complete control.

"My life hasn't always been easy, Ms. Waldron. Not by any stretch of the imagination. I know what it means to struggle. I know how it feels to beg for help that never comes. I've gone cold. So cold I've wrapped myself in plastic just to stay warm. I've been in the dark. Not because there was no electricity, but because I'd complained about deplorable conditions and was placed in a closet for hours. And I've gone hungry. More than once. I've been so hungry that I prayed to die in my sleep."

Gasps and whispers filled the room. Willow swallowed the lump of emotions forming in the back of her throat. Tears filled her eyes, and she blinked them away. Others in the room hadn't been able to wrangle their emotions, dabbing at their eyes with whatever was available.

When Willow slid a glance toward Chuck on the stage, she knew it was the best friend *and* the campaign manager admiring Lauder's courage. Chuck had earned several brownie points from her.

Lauder's voice drew her attention back to him. "You have a right to be unsure about me. I've never held public office. I'm inexperienced. And the fact remains that most of you don't know me from a jar of applesauce."

Willow laughed right along with the rest of the room. If he could bottle up and sell this rapport he had with people, he would be a billionaire.

Lauder continued. "To help you get to know me a little better, I could give you a rundown of my philanthropy resume, my involvement with A Hope for Home Foundation, which furnishes the first home of kids who've aged out of the foster system. I could tell you about my work with The Wright Foundation to help the disenfranchised in our communities develop job skills, learn trades, find affordable housing, obtain decent healthcare. I could even stand here and gush about my own organization, The Willow Tree Foundation."

His organization. Willow pushed her brows together. *The Willow Tree Foundation*? Something warm bloomed in her chest. Had he…? No, surely he hadn't named his foundation after her.

"I could rattle off the list of the countless other charities and foundations I support, but I won't. What I will do is ask you to trust me. Trust me when I tell you, all of you," he said, skimming the audience, "that I intend to fight like hell for children, seniors, our community, and that's not just a line I'm reading from some prepared speech. It's an absolute promise."

Lauder received a standing ovation. Applause thundered through the room. Willow's was the loudest. How the tide had turned. The same women who'd questioned his abilities earlier now chanted his name. And the same woman determined not to feel anything for him felt a whole lot.

Lauder couldn't recall ever shaking so many hands in his life. And he'd smiled so much his cheeks hurt. Plus, the hugs. These little old ladies sure liked to snatch you into their arms. He was fairly certain a few of those feisty women had copped feels on the sly.

He wasn't the only one garnering a lot of attention.

His gaze landed on Willow, laughing and chatting it up with a group of women. As if she'd sensed him ogling her, her head turned in his direction.

When she flashed him with one of those high-wattage smiles, dragonflies fluttered in his stomach. Only she could cause such an unwanted reaction. Locating Chuck among the crowd, he gave him the signal—a single nod—to wrap things up. He wanted some alone time with Willow. A need he should actually be avoiding, instead of pursuing.

After offering a final thank-you and saying goodbyes, Lauder escorted Willow to the waiting vehicle. Inside, he fell back against the black leather, removed his tie and draped it over his thigh. Unfastening the top two buttons of his shirt, he breathed a sigh of relief.

"The Willow Tree Foundation," she said.

How did he know that was coming? "Ah, yeah. I started it several years ago. Do you remember how we used to wish we could visit the beach or theme parks or countless other fun places?"

She nodded. "Yes."

"Well, that's what The Willow Tree Foundation does. We provide fun to foster kids, among other things. School supplies, clothing."

He waited for Willow to respond. A warm, but guarded, smile curled her lips. A look of admiration shone in her beautiful eyes.

"That's a noble cause," she said. Her gaze slid away. "And the name?"

Did she really need to ask? Playing into her inquiry, he said, "I wanted something that represented strength and beauty. A willow tree encompasses both those things. Plus, it was important to have a name that meant something to me." Once, she'd meant the entire world to him.

When Willow returned her attention to him, sentiment played on her lovely face. If it hadn't been clear before, he knew it was now, that she'd influenced the name of his foundation.

"A gala," she said.

He pressed his brows together. "What?"

"Remember how we also used to wish we were at one of those fancy galas we would watch on TV?"

Lauder chuckled. "I remember. I would wear an expensive tuxedo. You would wear a sapphire-blue gown. We would sip punch from fancy glasses and dance all night. I remember," he repeated.

"You should host a gala for the kids. They could wear fancy gowns and tuxedos that I'm sure local merchants wouldn't mind donating for such a great cause. Not to mention the publicity they would receive. How exciting would that be for the kids? It could also serve as a fundraiser for The Willow Tree Foundation." She shrugged. "Just think about it."

He would.

Willow pointed to the strip of fabric draped over his thigh. "You really don't like ties, do you?" she asked with laughter in her tone.

"No. It feels like a—"

Lauder paused, his eyes lowering to the hand Willow placed over her rumbling stomach. She burst out laughing, then apologized.

"Are you hungry?" he asked.

"Yes. I skipped breakfast this morning. I really wanted one of those Danishes back at the center, but people were sneezing, coughing and blowing their noses by them." She contorted her face the way a child might who'd just tasted a lemon for the first time.

Lauder gave a hard laugh. "That's exactly why I didn't get one. Why'd you skip breakfast?"

Willow's expression softened. "Nerves."

He pressed his brows together. "But earlier you said you weren't nervous."

"At that point, I wasn't."

Not fully understanding her statement, he still nodded. He'd dealt with his own bout of anxiousness himself. All night long he'd tossed and turned thinking about seeing Willow today. The first time in far too long. Even now, he couldn't believe how much he'd missed hearing her voice.

"Did you have breakfast?"

Lauder chuckled. "Oh, yeah." He never skipped a meal. Not if he could help it. Mostly because the pings of hunger brought back horrible memories, and partially because he liked to eat.

Willow jostled him. "Are you okay?"

"Yeah, yeah." He leaned forward and gave the driver an alternate destination, then eyed Willow. "I can't have you telling folks I sent you home hungry."

A mild look of caution spread across Willow's lightly made-up face. Her plum-painted lips curled into a hesitant smile. The urge to lean over and kiss her mouth made it hard to think clearly.

"I can grab leftovers at home," she said.

Lauder experienced a rush of panic at the idea of Willow getting away from him so soon. "No one likes leftovers. Plus, Chuck did say we should be seen in public together as much as possible." What in the hell was he doing? Why was he so determined to be near her? Hadn't he determined just a few days ago that Willow was bad for his mental and emotional health?

"Chuck said that, huh?" she said, barely audible.

"I'm being too presumptuous. You probably have plans for the remainder of your day. Don't let me ruin them."

"I don't."

His head jerked from the urgent response. Willow almost seemed embarrassed by her own eagerness. While her knee-jerk reaction may have bothered her, it did ego-stroking things to him. The idea of her wanting to spend time with him, too, was nice.

Willow manipulated the side of her neck, something he'd noticed she did when nervous. Why was she uneasy? Was she remembering the spastic way he'd acted the last time they were supposed to share a meal? Man, he still regretted the way he'd acted that night. He would make it up to her.

"Where are we going?" Willow asked.

"Comfort Foods. If that's okay with you."

"Sounds good."

As if he'd lost control of his eyes, they lowered to Willow's mouth as she talked about the good things she'd heard about the North Carolina staple. Watching her lips move made *his* stomach growl. And from past experience, he knew her kiss could satisfy his hunger.

"Is my lipstick smeared?"

Willow's words drew his attention from her mouth. The twinkle in her eye told him he'd been caught red-handed. Not that he'd been hiding. One corner of his mouth lifted. "No, you're perfect."

"No one's perfect," she said.

He begged to differ. When Willow slid her gaze away, he studied her profile. *You are perfect. So perfect for me. What in hell are you doing to me, woman?*

Chapter 10

Willow couldn't recall ever laughing as hard as she'd laughed the past hour. How could she have forgotten about Lauder's wacky sense of humor? Instead of it feeling like an hour with a man she hadn't seen in almost two decades, it had been more like talking to an old friend she chatted with every day.

She rested her elbows on the table, then propped her head in her hands and studied him.

"What?" he said, giving her one of those lopsided smiles.

If there were a way for him to offer them on the open market, even at a discounted price, he'd be rich. Well, richer. Hannah had done some independent research on Lauder. Turned out, Mr. Tolson had done extremely well for himself. And by well, she meant the man was a millionaire several times over. His commercial repurposing company had been a phenomenal success.

"Nothing," she said.

"There's something." He rested his forearms on the table and interlocked his fingers. "Tell me."

"You did great today. I'm proud of you." She believed in giving credit where credit was due.

"Thank you. That means a lot. Especially coming from you."

Willow arched a brow. "Coming from me?"

"You don't strike me as a woman who is easily impressed."

He was right, but had he been trying to impress her? "I can only imagine how hard it must have been sharing so much of yourself. It was just as hard to hear. I'm sorry you went through all of that, Lauder."

Lauder's eyes lowered to his now twiddling fingers. "What doesn't kill you makes you stronger, right?"

Before she realized what she was doing, Willow smothered Lauder's hands with hers. They eyed each other in comfortable silence.

"All right, folks. Did you save room for dessert?"

Reclaiming her hands, Willow faced the waitress. *Sam*, her name tag read. "There is always room for dessert. What do you recommend?"

The redhead talked with her hands. "Honey, we have a salted caramel bread pudding that will curl your toes."

Willow's head jerked. "Curl my toes, huh? Well, who could resist that?"

"One bread pudding." She turned toward Lauder. "What can I get you, Senator?"

Lauder gave a hearty laugh. "Not quite yet, but I hope."

"Well, you have my vote," Sam said. "Edmondson's smarmy."

Smarmy. Willow chuckled to herself. Interesting choice of word, but it fit. One thing Willow had noticed, Lauder's rival seemed to be unpopular.

"I appreciate that." He reached across the table and captured Willow's hand. "I'll just share this beautiful lady's bread pudding. If she'll allow me. Can't let her experience all that toe curling alone."

When Lauder brought her hand to his lips and kissed

the back, fire shot through her entire body. The space between her legs pounded so hard she was surprised their booth didn't vibrate. Squeezing her thighs together, she forced a smile. "Of course, sweetheart."

He kissed her fingers. Each one. Slowly and sensually. Her heart thumped in her chest, and her temperature rose several degrees. Oh, he knew how to dazzle.

Sam rested a hand on her chest. "You two are too darn adorable."

When Sam strolled away, Willow expected Lauder to release her hand. He didn't. "Um, Chuck would've approved of that performance," she said.

Lauder didn't respond. Each swipe of his thumb across her heated flesh sent a pulse through her system, further manipulating her already overactive core. If she pressed her thighs together any tighter, she was liable to cause damage.

"I owe you an apology, Willow."

"An…apology?" she said absently. "For what?"

"The other night…" His words trailed. "At my place."

Ignoring how Lauder's touch affected her, she said, "No apology necessary. If we had acted on temptation, it would have been a *huge* mistake." There was no other option but to downplay the entire situation. Her hand rested on her shoulder, but she removed it quickly.

Willow sent a quick thank-you up when Lauder's thumb movement halted. But a beat later, he started his sensual teasing again.

"Mistake," he said smoothly. "Really?"

"Yes."

"Huh." His eyes lowered to their joined hands. "Out of curiosity, why would it have been a mistake you think?"

Was he serious? He really needed to ask? "It would have further complicated our situation. A few moments of empty pleasure would have only blurred things. It's not like either of us is looking for anything serious, right?"

Finally, Lauder pulled away, but only because Sam placed a huge bowl in front of them.

"I added an extra scoop of homemade vanilla bean ice cream. You two enjoy," she said and was off again.

Willow's eyes widened. Sweets were definitely her weakness. "Wow. This looks amazing. I'm going to need—"

"Hours."

Willow's brow arched. "I'm sorry."

"You said a few moments of empty pleasure. In actuality, it would have been hours. Hours of *overflowing* gratification. I don't half-ass anything. Especially my lovemaking."

Willow's lips parted, but nothing flowed out. How in hell was she supposed to respond to something so… so arousing?

Lauder scooped up a heaping helping of the warm golden bread pudding and spooned it into his mouth. "Damn. That is good. Eat up. It'll make your toes curl."

Suddenly, it wasn't the bread pudding she had a taste for. Besides, she was fairly confident it couldn't satisfy the kind of hunger that dwelled inside her. Too bad Lauder was one treat she had to resist. She had a feeling he could be addictive. He was a habit she didn't need.

At 3:00 am, Lauder should have been fast asleep. Instead, he lay in bed eyeing the tendrils of light dancing across his ceiling, recalling his time with Willow the day before.

An image of her sitting in the front row at the McKimmon Center filled his head. *I'm right here.* She would never know how much her mouthing those three simple words had meant to him. *Simple?* No. Nothing about them had been simple. They'd been delicate but complex. Powerful, even. At least, mighty enough to anchor him.

That woman had worked the room like a pro, posing for every picture, shaking every hand. And she'd done it all with a smile on her face. Willow Dawson was truly a remarkable woman. Any man would be lucky to have her. He'd be lying if he said he hadn't thought about what it would be like to come home to Willow every night, instead of an empty house.

His loner lifestyle had never bothered him. It had been what he preferred. But since Willow had come on the scene, white picket fences were filtering into his thoughts more and more often. And kids. He'd never once imagined himself as a father. Now, he contemplated on what kind of father he would be. One thing was for sure, he'd be a much better father than his sperm donor had been, a man who'd gotten his wife—Lauder's mother—addicted to drugs, which had ultimately resulted in her overdose and death. He'd died several months later in the same manner.

Scattering it all from his head, he closed his eyes, only to have the lunch he and Willow shared torture him more. If he could have lounged in that booth all day gawking at her and holding her hand, he would have.

He could tell his daring comment about his lovemaking for hours had shaken her. If not by the discombobulated expression she flashed, then definitely by the fact she'd been as quiet as a chicken in a room full of sleeping foxes on the drive back to her place. Had she been annoyed he'd made such a bold and confident statement or had she been daydreaming about what it would have been like to spend hours in his bed?

The latter caused a tightening in his gut. Hell, he'd fantasized about making love to Willow so many times he was surprised that the mere sight of her didn't cause an erection. How was it possible to want one woman so damn much?

This shit was killing him, and not softly. This desire for Willow that grew increasingly more intense each time he was within feet of her. It felt as if he were sparring with destiny every time he denied just how much she was in his system. And if that was the case, did it make sense to prolong what was already fated?

A mistake?

The insult had stung like salt poured into an open wound. That was until he realized she hadn't believed it was a mistake no more than he had. *That hand on her neck.* A dead giveaway. She'd been saving face. Which suggested she felt ashamed in some way for yearning for him so vehemently. She'd wanted him just as much as he'd wanted her. *Still* wanted her.

But it wasn't an empty moment of pleasure he wanted. He wanted far more. And that scared him. What if they didn't work out? He wasn't sure his heart could take losing her again.

After all of this time, he could still recall how it had felt when Willow had pushed him away. That experience had taught him a valuable lesson about attachments. Don't. Form. Them. It had been a rule he'd always obeyed.

Until now.

Until Willow.

Chapter 11

Willow had come to the conclusion that if she ate one more chicken dinner, she'd cluck. Lauder had referred to the countless political dinners they'd attended the past couple of weeks as the Rubber Chicken Circuit. It hadn't taken her long to understand why.

The dinners had all been at the personal residences of some of Lauder's most influential campaign donors. The menus had all consisted of some variation of chicken: marsala, parmigiana, herbed and baked, cordon bleu. With the exception of one or two, most of the dishes tasted as though they'd been prepared the week before, frozen, then microwaved and served the night of the event.

Thankfully, instead of pulling up the driveway of a sprawling estate, they were attending a musical at the Duke Energy Center for the Performing Arts in downtown Raleigh. Like each time they made a public appearance, Lauder was bombarded by folks greeting him, assuring their support and requesting pictures. Lots and lots of pictures. All of which he dutifully entertained.

Their location in the balcony of the hall reminded Willow of her trip to the opera several years back. The only difference, in the New York theater there were others occupying the space alongside her. Here, she and Lauder were the only ones in the section. Surely, more people would join them.

Had it not been for the fact that the seats below in the mezzanine, orchestra and dress circle zones were teeming with people, she would have assumed they were way early for the performance.

"You think anyone else will be joining us?" she asked with a laugh.

"No," Lauder said.

Her brows bunched. Clearly, Lauder took it as his cue to explain.

"I ensured we'd be alone here."

Alone? Alarm filtered into her system. "Why?" Not that being alone with him was such a bad thing.

"I wanted you to be able to enjoy the show without interruption."

Willow considered the cost associated with Lauder's act. There were easily seventy-five seats in their section, and the tickets for the show started well over a hundred dollars. "You didn't have to do that, Lauder. Thank you. That was very thoughtful." But who would have really disturbed them during a musical to take pictures, or talk politics?

"I'm a thoughtful kind of guy," he said, followed by one of those dazzling smiles.

They eyed each other in comfortable silence for a moment.

"I'm not sure I would have pegged you as a musical type of guy," she said, dousing the rising heat from his stare.

"Oh, trust me, I'm not. I'm only here to fulfill a promise."

Again, Willow was confused.

"The summer musical," Lauder said as if it should have meant something to her. "At the high school," he added.

Awareness set in. How could she have forgotten? That was the day she'd decided she wanted Lauder to be her first. "Oh, my God. I can't believe you remember that."

"Some things you can't forget," he said. "Like how you watched the performers on stage that day with such amazement, and the wide smile that lit your face for the entire two-hour performance. I'm not sure I'd ever seen you so happy. I could never forget that."

Willow smiled softly. "You promised to one day take me to a real musical, where we'd sit in the balcony and pretend to be royalty."

Lauder swept his hand through the air. "Here we are, my queen," he said in a borrowed accent. "I don't like to break promises."

The lights dimmed before Willow could respond, which wasn't such a bad thing, because she had no idea what to say. A simple thank-you didn't seem powerful enough.

Lauder slid his attention toward the stage. She studied his handsome profile. He'd remembered that day. After all this time.

Business. Just business, she reminded herself when something warm swirled in the pit of her stomach.

Willow faced the stage, but brought her gaze back to Lauder. "It wasn't what was happening on stage that caused the smile," she said.

Lauder eyed her. "What was it?"

"You sliding your hand into mine. I had been quietly wishing you would."

She recalled the goose bumps that had prickled her skin when he'd smoothly captured her hand and rested his damp palm against hers. Her cheeks were sore the next day from smiling so hard.

"Huh," Lauder said, returning his attention to the stage. Willow followed suit.

A beat later, he reached over and captured her hand. She tensed from the unexpected move, but relaxed when she tossed him an urgent glance and saw the humorous grin on his face.

"Ha, ha," she said.

His fingers tightened as if he expected her to pull away. It had crossed her mind, because his touch—like lava—was threatening to melt her.

Unlike years ago, Lauder's palm was bone-dry, letting her know he was not the nervous boy from her past. But that was the only thing that was different. The move still made her smile and still made her want him.

Willow scowled at Hannah, then hurled a chunk of the polymer clay she was kneading at her. Not because what Hannah had said was untrue—Willow wholeheartedly agreed that she could be overly cautious—but because she just didn't want to hear it. It was like a church sermon where your toes were the ones being crushed.

"Did you forget the arrangement I'm in? Is that not daring enough? Especially for me."

"Yes, that's plenty daring, but you always take risks in your *professional* life. And this arrangement falls in the business category. What I'm talking about is your *personal* life."

Willow considered reminding Hannah of her past friends-with-benefits arrangement with Reggie. That was rash, right? Ha. Who was she kidding? She was a full-fledged prude.

Hannah closed the distance between them and leaned

against Willow's sculpting table. "You want to sleep with Lauder. I know you do. Or at least, you should want to after the trip to the musical. It sounds so romantic. Him fulfilling a twenty-year-old promise. And the holding hand part. So romantic."

"It wasn't romantic, Cupid, it was business." *Just business*, she repeated to herself, despite it feeling like so much more. But that *so much more* was what she had to ignore.

Hannah brushed Willow's words off. "Since you've officially ended things with Reggie, you need a new bed buddy. Lauder seems like the perfect candidate to me."

When Hannah snickered, Willow rolled her eyes away. Considering her valiant words, she scoffed. *The audacity.* It only grated her nerves because again, Hannah had been right. She wanted to sleep with Lauder.

Willow released her sexual frustrations out on the mound of clay she'd been kneading for the past half hour. It didn't typically take this long to soften it, but her mind wasn't fully on the facial reconstruction project.

"All I'm saying, Will, is live a little. You're young, beautiful and financially stable. Enjoy life. Be spontaneous. Be a little irresponsible, wild, hasty."

"When I tried to be all of those things, I was shot down, remember?" Bruising her pride in the process. "Besides, he also agreed that it would be a huge mistake for us to get involved, remember?" Those hadn't been his exact words, but if her stretch of the truth got Hannah off her back, she'd roll with it.

"Strictly business, huh?" Hannah said.

Willow refocused on the task at hand. "Yes. *Strictly* business. He could be considered my boss. I would never sleep with my boss." Had she really just called Lauder her boss? Well, again, if it got Hannah off her back, she'd roll with it.

"Whatever. So what event do you have today with Mr. Strictly Business?"

"The next one isn't until next month. Meet the Media." She rolled her eyes heavenward. That was not an event she was looking forward to. All the prying reporters and their invasive questions. The whole concept made her stomach knot.

"Really? Huh. So… I guess if there's no 'business' reason for him to be here, then it must be personal."

"What are you—"

Hannah directed Willow with her head. When Willow turned, her entire body went into self-preservation mode. *Lauder?* What was he doing here?

"And he comes bearing gifts," Hannah said out the side of her mouth.

"Shut up," Willow said, mimicking Hannah's side-mouth chatting method.

"Ladies."

The scent of Lauder's cologne tantalized Willow. "H—" Her words caught. Clearing her throat, she said, "Hey. What are you doing here?"

"Hi," Hannah said, grinning from ear to ear. "Beautiful flowers."

Lauder slid his appraising gaze from Willow and eyed Hannah. "I'm glad you think so, because they're for you."

Hannah rested a hand on her chest. "For…me?"

"Yes. Kind of a bribe. I want to steal Willow away for a little while."

Hannah accepted the colorful bouquet. "Thank you. Take her. Keep her as long as you like. Excuse me while I place these in water."

No, she didn't. Willow shook her head at Hannah's disloyalty. And over a dang bouquet of flowers.

Once Hannah ambled away, Lauder slid his gaze back to Willow. "So, are you up for hanging out with me for a couple of hours?"

Couple of hours? Willow fixed her mouth to craft some ridiculous excuse, but changed her mind, reminding herself that spending time with him went along with their agreement. Plus, Hannah was wrong. She could be adventuresome. "Give me five minutes while I clean up?"

Lauder seemed surprised at how easy that had been.

He nodded. "I'll be right here." His eyes slid to the partially clay-covered skull on the table. "On second thought, I'll wait in the reception area."

She laughed. "Okay."

Several minutes later, Willow and Lauder left the building. "So, to what do I owe this surprise outing?"

Lauder slid his hands into his black suit pants. "Well, Chuck suggested I take you someplace nice."

A ping of disappointment taunted her. "Oh. So, Chuck sent you?"

"No. He merely made the suggestion. Coming was all me."

"I see. And why would he make such a suggestion? Does he want us to get more exposure together?" she said.

"Yes, he does, actually. But that's not the purpose of this outing. Chuck says you have me trending."

Willow stopped walking. "Trending? How?"

"He's unequivocally convinced your idea to use my past is what sold me to the seniors. Different media outlets are posting pics they took of us on Instagram, Twitter, Facebook. Folks are tweeting, sharing, liking and tagging like crazy."

Lauder shook his head as though it was all too surreal. She, on the other hand, found nothing at all out of the ordinary about it. Folks had simply discovered what she already knew. Lauder was the best man for the job.

Starting to walk again, Willow said, "I'm not sure I had *that* much to do with it. Your passionate delivery was what touched their hearts." Because it had certainly touched hers.

"Yeah, but I never would have tapped into that dark place had you not been there. In the front row. Just like you'd promised. Thank you."

A smile touched her lips. "You're welcome."

Willow broke their connection before his probing eyes witnessed more than they should. "Um, so where are we headed?" she asked, reaching Lauder's dark gray Infiniti SUV. Again, the vehicle suited him. Sleek, powerful and demanding appreciation.

Lauder opened her door and waited for her to settle inside. Once she had, he rounded the front of the vehicle, winking at her on his way to the driver's side. Sliding behind the wheel, he said, "Hemming's Steakhouse on Glenwood. Have you ever been?"

"No." But she'd heard great things about the food at the five-star establishment. Plus, one of the local news outlets had mentioned their perfect one hundred sanitation grade on the channel's restaurant ratings segment.

"I would have preferred this be a dinner date, but I have to be at the airport in a couple of hours. I didn't want to wait to show my gratitude."

Ignoring his use of the word *date*, she said, "Airport?" To her own ear, it sounded as though she'd never heard of such a place.

"I have to travel to Memphis for business. I'll only be gone a couple of days," he said as if he expected Willow to miss him.

"Ah. You fly commercial?"

Lauder chuckled. "Yes. Is that hard to believe?"

"No. I just assumed you would have your own private jet."

This time Lauder barked a throaty laugh. "You really do have a lot to learn about me. About *me*," he emphasized. "Not the businessman, not the politician."

"Are they that different?"

"Like night and day."

"I'm intrigued."

Lauder flashed a wicked grin that piqued her curiosity. *What do you have up your sleeve?*

Obviously, the universe was on their side, because they found excellent parking. The inside of Hemming's was fashioned in aged wood. The smell of spices and fresh bread stirred her appetite. Autographed pictures of celebrity patrons plastered several walls.

Lauder was recognized by quite a few people inside the bustling restaurant. Graciously, he shook hands and posed for pictures. *The perfect candidate*, a middle-aged woman labeled him, then assured him he had her vote. To that, Lauder flashed her one of his lethal smiles.

Lauder requested the most secluded table in the restaurant, which only made Willow more curious about what he had up his sleeve. Maybe she was being paranoid. Maybe he'd simply chosen this location to be away from the crowd, away from disturbances like at the musical they'd attended.

But why?

Did he have a bombshell to drop on her, or simply wanted her all to himself?

That made her laugh, and she settled on the former, believing the latter was mere wishful thinking.

Well, if he had outrageous news to share, it couldn't

hold as much shock value as him asking her to be his make-believe lover. That made her breathe a bit easier.

The entirety of the meal, Willow expected Lauder to drop whatever bomb she had an idea he'd been lugging. Nothing. They simply chatted and laughed. Conversation with him was so effortless that it was spooky.

After leaving the restaurant, Lauder drove Willow back to her office. He pulled into a space, put the vehicle in Park and shut off the engine. But instead of exiting, he shifted his solid frame toward her.

Uh-oh. Here it comes.

"You were right the other week. Neither one of us is looking for anything serious."

"Okay."

"We've both made sacrifices to make this thing we're doing work."

This *thing*? Didn't he mean this ruse? This ploy. This scheme. "Sure."

"Including sex."

The mention of sex garnered her urgent focus. "Uh-huh." Where the heck was this conversation headed?

Lauder chortled. "I'm not sure about you, but I miss it. A lot."

Oh, she most definitely did, too, but wasn't about to confess it aloud.

"I propose we add another dynamic to our arrangement. Make-believe lovers with benefits. Absolutely no strings."

For several seconds, all she could do was blink dumbly with her lips parted but nothing escaping.

"I can see I've stunned you speechless. Don't answer now. Take some time to think about it. Let me know your answer when I return. If it's no, I'll understand. I just thought this would benefit the both of us."

Nope, she hadn't dreamed this conversation, which

had been her first thought. For lack of a better reaction, she nodded clumsily. Lauder made a move to open his door. "I can walk myself inside. You have a catch to plane. *A plane to catch*," she corrected, then fumbled with the door handle. "Thank you for lunch. Have a safe trip."

"I hope—"

Lauder was midthought when Willow closed the door. *Shoot.* She made a move to open it, reconsidered, then made another motion to open it but changed her mind again. With an exhausted huff, she took off toward the building.

Inside the elevator, she jabbed at the button as if doing so would make the doors close faster. She gnawed at the corner of her lip. *Make-believe lovers with benefits.* Had Lauder really just asked her to...

Nah. The only logical explanation was that she'd dreamed it. She'd dreamed it all. But hadn't she already established it hadn't been in her head? Pinching herself—just to make sure she wasn't actually in a state of slumber—she winced.

Nope, she was wide-awake, which made his proposal even more confusing, because not too long ago, he'd been the one who'd said their sleeping together couldn't happen.

Several hours later, Willow stood outside Lauder's hotel room in Memphis. She'd decided to give him her answer in person. Thanks to Chuck, she'd gotten all the details she'd needed to make this impromptu trip. He'd also agreed not to tell Lauder she was coming.

Overly cautious my big toe.

Willow raised her hand but stopped shy of knocking, her burst of confidence dwindling quickly. *I can do this. It's no different than what I had with Reggie.*

Lies. All lies.

It was different. Completely different. She'd never had

a hint of feelings for Reggie. Lauder… She sighed, not wanting to admit how he'd grown on her. Like unmanageable kudzu that you can't get rid of. Despite how much she'd weeded him from her thoughts, he still found his way back.

Just do it! They were both grown and they'd both be getting what they needed. They'd both suffer the fallout if things went sideways. She didn't allow that to dissuade her. Even if it were only once, she wanted to be with Lauder. She'd deal with any repercussions later.

Before her knuckles made contact with the door, her cell phone rang. Willow yelped, then stepped aside. Placing her overnight bag down, she fished the phone from her purse and swiped her finger across the screen. In a muted tone, she said, "You nearly gave me a heart attack."

"You must be up to no good," Hannah said with a snicker.

"I haven't gotten the chance yet."

"What? You've been in Memphis over an hour."

Willow rested her palm against her forehead. Yes, she'd been there over an hour, but it had taken her thirty minutes to build up the nerve to enter the elevator. Another minute or two to press the button to the twelfth floor and a couple more to actually step out of the metal box.

"I was just about to knock when you called. Maybe your call was a sign. The universe's way of telling me I'm making a huge mistake."

"Quit making excuses. Get off this phone, knock on that door, take that bull by the horns and ride him into the sunset."

"You're—"

Willow paused when Lauder's hotel room door opened. Her lungs seized when she heard a woman's voice. Whipping around so that her back faced them, she stood frozen in place.

"Willow?" Hannah said. "Willow," she repeated. "What's wrong? Say something, dammit."

"Shhh," she hissed into the phone.

Lauder started to say something to the woman, but paused midsentence. "Willow?"

Shit. Okay, play it cool. She slowly turned to face them, the phone still pressed to her ear. "Oh, hey, um… Lauder." Her eyes slid to the gorgeous brown-skinned woman standing beside him. "And Lauder's female friend."

"Female friend!" Hannah blurted in Willow's ear.

Willow lowered the phone, sure both Lauder and his friend had heard Hannah's outburst.

Lauder's brow furrowed. "Willow…what are you doing in Memphis?"

"What am I doing in Memphis?" she said. The real question was, what was he *really* doing in Memphis. Willow tossed another glance in his companion's direction. *Business my ass.* "Um…"

Seeing Lauder with another woman angered her. Not because she was jealous or anything—well, she had to admit, she was a little heated seeing them together. But it was mainly because she'd given up her means of sexual relief—i.e., Reggie—while Lauder obviously thought he could fly to another state to fulfill his needs.

Some nerve. To think she'd actually believed him when he'd said he'd given up sex. She should have known better. Apparently, having her as his local lay was more convenient for the times when he couldn't make it to Memphis. Here she was, again, allowing Lauder Tolson to make a fool out of her. How could she have been so damn stupid? *Never again*, she promised herself.

"What am I doing in Memphis?" she repeated again, her words a bit sharper than she'd intended.

He nodded slowly. "Yes, that was the question."

Tempted to blast him right there in the hallway, she reconsidered. No way would she let him know how much he'd hurt her. That seemed to be the only thing he ever had for her...hurt. "You asked a question before you left North Carolina. I'd wanted to give you my answer in person. Obviously, I've caught you at a bad time, so I'll go."

"No, I should go. To my own room. Let you two handle...whatever this is." Lauder's female companion stuck her hand out toward Willow. "I'm Dreena, by the way. My *boss*," she emphasized, "seems a bit too awestruck and dazzled to make a proper introduction."

Boss? She was one of Lauder's employees. A wave of relief, regret and shame rippled through Willow.

"Willow," she said, shaking Dreena's hand. "Nice to meet you."

Turning to a still-silent Lauder, Dreena said, "I'm ordering room service." She clapped Lauder on the shoulder. "A porterhouse. And an expensive bottle of wine."

Then she was gone, leaving Willow and Lauder alone in the hallway, staring at each other.

Hannah's squawking drew Willow's attention. Placing the phone back to her ear, she said, "I'll call you back," then ended the call. Softening her tone considerably, she said, "I should have called or not have come at all. It was a rash and obviously stupid decision. I didn't mean to—"

"You thought Dreena and I were more than friends. You were jealous," he said with a straight face.

"Jealous?" She released a nervous laugh. "*Psh*. I wasn't jealous. That's absolutely—"

Lauder backed her against the cream-colored wall and kissed her hard. Once the shock wore off, she parted her lips and allowed his tongue to explore the inside of her mouth. The kiss was so deliciously satisfying, she went weak in the knees.

Pulling away, he said, "You were jealous."

"A little." Damn, had she really just confessed to being jealous?

"A little, huh?"

"Barely even noticeable."

"Uh-huh." He pushed a lock of hair behind her ear. "So, what's your answer?"

Willow's mouth gaped. Was he serious? Hadn't she just flown nearly four hours to be here? With him. Plus, she'd just made out with him in the middle of a hotel hallway. Could he really not know what her answer was? "It's not that difficult to figure out, Lauder."

"I don't want to figure it out. I want to hear you say it, Willow."

"What exactly is it you want to hear?"

Resting a hand above her head, he leaned in close again and whispered in her ear, "I want to *hear* you call my name. Over and over and over again."

Willow drew in a sharp breath as though the words had startled her.

Lauder pressed closer to her. "I want to hear you moan in absolute pleasure. I want to hear you tell me—no, beg me—not to stop. And I want to hear it all night long." He rested a hand on her waist. "But right now, I'll settle for hearing you say you want me."

"I want you." Stunned that the words had come so quickly, so easily, she swallowed hard. "I mean—"

"You said exactly what you meant." He brushed a finger across her cheek. "Didn't you?"

"Yes," she said like an obedient child.

Chapter 12

Dreena had been 100 percent accurate. Lauder had been awestruck, dazzled, dazed, consumed and a million other terms for stunned as hell one could come up with. But more important, he was ecstatic. On the outside, he appeared to be in complete control. On the inside, however, a storm raged. One that could only be calmed by making unhurried love to Willow, which he intended to do.

The fact that she'd flown all this way to see him, to be with him, did crazy things to his body. Things, again, only she'd be able to remedy. Lauder's heart pounded against his rib cage like a triathlete who'd just sprinted across the finish line in first place. With one hand, he collected the small bag by Willow's feet, then inched her forward with the other.

Inside, Willow's eyes darted around the one-bedroom suite. From the cream-and-turquoise walls, to the fully equipped kitchen, living area, and workstation littered with papers.

"Nice," she said.

"Why don't you make yourself at home, look around. I need to step out a quick second."

Willow's brow furrowed. "Where are you going?"

He chuckled. "I wasn't prepared for you." He needed protection.

Awareness lit her gorgeous face, then she nodded.

He never practiced unsafe sex, but if Willow had told him to take her right then, he would have abandoned all common sense. She gnawed at the corner of her lip, and he was tempted to snatch her into his arms and kiss her delirious, but he fought the desire. "I'll be right back."

On his way out of the room, he snagged the ball cap he'd packed. While he doubted anyone in Memphis would recognize him, he couldn't be too careful.

Lauder damn near ran to the elevator, jabbing the down button in quick succession as though doing so would make the doors open any faster. A ding finally sounded the arrival, and Lauder grew all giddy inside. Entering the elevator, he stabbed at the button that would take him to the lower level.

Finally. He sprinted across the lobby, out the main entrance and toward the drugstore on the corner. He prayed they were still open at near nine in the evening. *Yes*, he thought when he saw the glowing OPEN sign. Before entering, he pulled the cap even lower on his head. All he needed was a picture of him purchasing a box of condoms in Memphis plastered all over the front page of the *N&O*.

In and out, Lauder hurried back to the suite. Inside, he heard the shower running. Entering the bedroom, he tossed all four boxes of magnum condoms on the nightstand. Creeping to the bathroom door, he eased inside.

Steam filled the room, but the silhouette of Willow's body through the fogged-up glass shower door was unmistakable. Her every move proved to test his resolve. *Join her* played in his head, but he resisted the strong force pulling him toward the enclosure.

Instead, he snagged a towel from the rack and propped

himself against the marble countertop and waited. She hummed a catchy melody, one he was sure he'd heard before but couldn't quite put his finger on.

Several minutes later, she shut off the water and stepped out, clearly oblivious to his presence. The air seized in his chest at the sight of her magnificent body. *Flawless.* Apparently sensing his presence, Willow's head snapped up. To his benefit, she didn't make a single move to hide her body from him, suggesting she was comfortable in her own skin. He liked that.

"You're back" was all she said.

He didn't say a word, simply approached her with the towel in hand. Starting at her shoulders, he took his time drying her skin. Her arms. Her breasts. Her torso. Each swipe of the plush fabric tightened the knot in his stomach.

Willow trembled. He could feel it through the towel. There would be a lot more quivering in her near future. Of course, he didn't give the warning aloud. Continuing in silence, he lowered to his knees, dried one leg, then the other. He ignored the proximity of his face to the patch of curly black hairs covering her mound. All it would take was a tilt of his head to savor what he wanted so badly.

Not yet.

He was hard.

Too damn hard.

So damn hard it felt as if his skin would rip.

Returning to a full stand, he tossed the towel aside and scooped Willow into his arms. A yelp escaped her lips. They eyed each other in piping hot silence. He wanted to kiss her. Yearned to kiss her.

Not yet.

Carrying her to the bed, he eased her down like a priceless doll. He stood at the edge of the bed, his eyes combing over every bare inch of her. The more he drank her in, the thirstier he grew. "Damn, woman. Do you have any idea the effect you're having on me?"

Her eyes burned a slow line down his body, stopping at his crotch. A gentle smile touched her lips, either amused or impressed by the bulge there.

"Doesn't seem fair that you're still dressed, and I'm so…exposed," she said.

"What's unfair is the way you have my heart banging in my chest from anticipation."

"Well, I guess that makes us even."

"Not by any means. You haven't even begun to see my retribution."

Willow came up on her knees and grabbed the hem of the white button-down shirt he wore. Starting at the bottom, she unfastened each button. When she was done, she swept the loose fabric over his shoulders. A beat later, her entire body went still staring at the image on his left pec. With her lips parted, she raised her eyes to his.

"It's the only thing I had left of you," he said.

Willow's trembling fingers glided over the dragonfly tattoo he'd gotten what seemed like an eternity ago.

"You did this for me?"

He nodded. "I came back for you, Willow."

"You came back for me? What does that mean?"

"Shortly after my eighteenth birthday. I didn't know how, but I was determined to make you forgive me and convince you to come away with me." He brushed a finger down her cheek. "I was too late. You had left for college."

"You came back for me?" Her expression suggested she couldn't believe what she'd just heard. "Did—" Her words caught. "Did anyone tell you where I'd gone?"

"Yes. I couldn't afford to get to Atlanta. Then reality set in. If I couldn't even afford to get to you, how in hell could I afford to provide for you? You deserved so much more than I could offer, so I chose to let you go." He placed his hand over the one Willow had resting on his chest. "But I needed a piece of you."

A tear trickled down Willow's cheek. She shook her head. "I would have gone with you anywhere. As long as it was with you, I wouldn't have minded the struggle."

It wasn't until that second that Lauder realized just how much Willow still lingered in his heart. He cradled her face, then kissed her with the urgency and force of rushing water. He was determined to sweep her away in his current.

Feeling her all the way to his bones, he deepened the kiss, her moans encouraging him to give more, take more. The game had changed for them.

They'd agreed to play by a noncommittal set of rules. No way could he honor that. Not even if he wanted to. This woman had a serious hold on him. He'd gotten Willow back, and he'd be damned if he ever lost her again. Forget all the rules. He was playing for keeps. She just didn't know it yet.

Willow didn't want the power-packed lip-lock to ever end. Lauder's beautiful words, coupled with the way he was kissing her senseless, had her body—scratch that, her soul—on fire. A slow burn that he controlled.

He snatched away from her mouth and stared hard into her eyes. "Has Ramon ever kissed you like that?"

She laughed. "*Reggie*. And no. We never kissed." They'd been strictly sex, nothing more. Once they'd both gotten what they'd needed, each went their separate ways. Yes, at times it felt cold, especially in those instances when she could have used warm arms wrapped around her, but she'd known all along Reggie's arms weren't the ones for her.

"Never?"

She shook her head.

"Why?"

"Because I never wanted to kiss him."

Impatiently, she dipped forward to taste him again, but Lauder pulled away. A second later, he grinned. Placing his hand under her chin—obviously to control the situation—he kissed one corner of her mouth, then the other. It was the most arousing thing ever.

"But you want to kiss me?" he asked.

"Yes." Why lie?

Lauder pecked her gently, nipped her bottom lip, then dragged his tongue over it. She sucked his teasing tongue into her mouth. His hands explored her body, across her shoulders, along her rib cage. Over her butt, where he squeezed not so gently. It felt oh so good.

Lauder inched her back on the bed, blanketing her body with his. Bringing their connection to an end, his lips grazed her ear. "I'm going to kiss your lobe."

His lips brushed against her, causing her skin to prickle.

"I'm going to kiss your jaw."

Another kiss.

"I'm going to kiss your lips."

A third kiss.

"I'm going to kiss your chin."

Indeed, he did.

"I'm going to kiss your beautiful neck."

Several more kisses feathered her skin.

Raising his head, he looked into her eyes. "I'm going to kiss your breasts, then drag my tongue down your torso and plant my face between your thighs. I'm going to make you come. Harder than you've ever come before. Then I'm going to enter you, nice and slow. But before any of that happens, I'm going to finish undressing."

Willow released a shaky laugh. "Hurry. Please."

Damn. Was she begging? *Yes!* To hell with pride. She wanted what she wanted. And what she wanted was Lauder. All of him.

Dizzy with anticipation, Willow sobered when Lauder lowered his boxers. Her eyes widened, appreciating both his length and girth. Reggie had been sufficiently endowed, but Lauder… The man had truly been blessed by the gods.

The tips of her fingers tingled to touch him, stroke him. She bit into the corner of her lip. Never in her life had she ever experienced such a heightened state of arousal. Every inch of Lauder's body was magnificent. Strong legs. Toned chest. Sculpted arms. Every inch…perfect.

The feel of Lauder's bare flesh against hers when he covered her body again caused unexplainable emotions to swirl inside her. Their combined energy—raw, potent—proved too much for her system to handle. A tear slid from the corner of her eye.

Lauder swiped his thumb across her cheek. "What is that about?"

Willow swallowed hard. "I don't know." It was an honest answer. She had no idea why being here with Lauder made her so emotional. It was like experiencing a million intense sensations all at once. And she welcomed each one of them.

How was Lauder causing her system to spark on so many cylinders, especially when all he'd done was kiss her? Instantly, she retracted her prior statement. This man had done far more than kiss her. He'd opened a locked chamber in her heart she desperately wanted to keep him from entering.

But she couldn't.

Dammit.

She couldn't.

Lauder's mouth closed over hers. The unhurried manner in which he savored her further aggravated whatever this was she was experiencing. His relaxed tongue swept every inch of her mouth. When his hand cupped one of her breasts and squeezed, she moaned with delight.

"Mmm. I like that sound," Lauder said against their joined mouths.

Breaking their connection, he kissed a trail between the valley of her breasts. His warm lips teased one of her taut, achy nipples, while he rolled the other between his fingers. The space between her legs throbbed. She needed his touch, his lips, his tongue, something to provide the release she direly needed.

How was he able to remain so damn composed? Maybe he did this a lot. The idea of any other woman getting any piece of Lauder angered her. But the resentment faded when his tongue made a slow descent down her body.

Unable to control it, her body shivered as if she were standing outside during the dead of winter. *How?* she asked herself. *How was he—*

Lauder's stiff tongue circled her clit, then suckled her tenderly. Her cries tore through the room. "Oh…my— Yes!" Her chest rose and fell in rapid successions. "Yes! Right there."

Then he stopped.

"No!" Her head jutted forward, the room spinning around her. "What—"

Lauder bent her legs toward her chest and placed her

hands behind her knees. A beat later, he lowered his head again. His arms encircled her thighs, and he pulled her closer to his mouth. He seemed determined to conquer her.

And he did.

But she didn't just break, she shattered into a thousand tiny shards. Not a single inch of her body was spared the pleasure Lauder provided. Even her scalp experienced a cooling sensation. Her hands fell from her legs, but Lauder replaced them, pressing her knees even closer to her chest, continuing the expert use of his tongue.

Her neck arched, causing the crown of her head to dig into the pillow.

Her fingers clenched.

Her back curved.

Her legs shook.

Her toes curled.

On the heels of the last orgasm, another electrifying shockwave tore through her. This one so powerful her lungs seized. She swore she'd suffocate from her inability to breathe. Luckily, Lauder released her from his paralyzing grip, kissing his way back to her mouth.

"You should have warned me," he said, pecking her once, then twice.

"About?" she managed to ask.

"How divine you taste."

Lauder crashed his mouth to hers, preventing whatever response she would have had to his statement. Unlike their last kiss, this one was urgent, untamed. Their tongues sparred, teased, taunted, then meshed into a beautiful harmony. The moment transitioned from critical to delicate.

Peeling his mouth away, Lauder peppered kisses to her ear. "You're hazardous, Weeping Willow," he whispered.

"I hate that name," she said too sensually to be convincing. "And why am I hazardous?"

Lauder's head rose. He regarded her as if she should have known the answer. Maybe she did have an idea, ridiculous as it was. But was believing he still cared about her after all of this time that farfetched? It was clear something was happening between them. Something… real. But for now, there were no strings attached and she was okay with that.

Lauder slid his hard stare away, retrieved one of the unopened boxes of condoms on the dresser and ripped into it. Removing one of the foils, he sheathed himself, then reclaimed her mouth.

Instead of entering her all at once, he eased inside inch by delicious inch, filling her, stretching her. Willow whimpered, pushing her hips forward to claim more of him. Again, Lauder controlled the situation, only giving her what he wanted her to have. But hadn't he warned that he planned to enter her nice and slow? A man of his word.

"More, Lauder. Please." *Ugh*. When had she become so sexually needy? Willow answered her own question. The second Lauder touched her.

"Someone is hungry," he said, kissing the corner of her mouth.

"Starving. Feed me."

Lauder gave one sharp thrust forward, then stilled. Willow cried out and yearned for more. A moan rumbled deep in Lauder's chest. A second later, he withdrew. A second after that, he thrust forward again, hitting a spot inside her that sent a shiver through her entire body.

"I know how I want to give it to you," he said, giving her a rough kiss. Tearing his mouth away, he continued, "But tell me how you want it. And don't be bashful."

Bashful? Ha! Bashful went out the window the second he'd buried his face between her legs. "You have my body screaming for hard and fast, but it's also craving slow and gentle."

Without saying a word, Lauder took charge, moving in and out of her with slow and gentle strokes. He rotated his hips, hitting pleasure spots she had no idea even existed until now. Just as her body conformed to Lauder's smooth movement, he switched it up, delivering long, hard, fast strokes. Willow thought she would lose her mind. She whimpered, moaned, called his name.

She held on.

She let go.

She submitted.

Then…he stopped, reverting to slow and gentle. Over the next several minutes, he alternated back and forth. Hard, fast. Slow, gentle. Willow dutifully rode this wave of intense pleasure, but when Lauder placed her legs over his shoulders and drove himself so deep inside her she swore she could feel him in her chest, she crumbled.

His swift and steady momentum grew sluggish and clumsy. After several more pumps, he growled, then throbbed inside her. The feel of his pounding release sent her over the edge again.

"Shit." Lauder forced the word through clenched teeth, collapsing half on the bed, half on Willow. "Shit," he repeated, burying his damp forehead in the crook of her neck.

Willow could feel Lauder's heart pounding in his chest with the same intensity as her own. Normally, this would have been the moment she got out of the bed, dressed and went home. That wasn't exactly an option now.

For one, she was eight hundred miles from home. For two, she wasn't 100 percent confident her legs would support an escape from Lauder's bed. For three…she held no desire to leave.

Chapter 13

The following morning, Willow awoke to the sound of thunder. Dazed, she glanced around the room. It took her a moment to recall her whereabouts. *Memphis*. With Lauder. A soothing warmth spread over her.

The sound of the shower drew her attention to the closed bathroom door, then the bedside clock. *Six?* That explained why she was tired. It had been well after 4 a.m. before she and Lauder had fallen asleep.

Well, before she had fallen asleep. She wasn't sure what time Lauder had dozed off or if he'd actually fallen asleep at all. The last thing she remembered was him pulling her close to his chest and securing her in a protective hold. A short time after, she'd dozed off to the sound of his thudding heartbeat and the feel of his hand caressing her arm.

Nestling back under the covers, Willow closed her eyes. But instead of finding sleep, she found herself reliving her night with Lauder. The man was a phenomenal lover, who'd made it his mission to please and fulfill her. And good gracious, had he. Countless times.

The more he offered, the more she'd wanted, needed, greedily accepted. It was like she'd been unable to get enough of him. But clearly, she hadn't been the only one who couldn't seem to get her fill.

They'd shared such a beautiful night together, but what exactly were they doing? Yes, they'd both agreed to no strings. So why did she feel so tangled, so bound? And why did she like the feeling so much?

Lost in thought, she didn't realize Lauder had ended his shower until the bathroom door creaked open. A surge of untamed arousal jolted her body to life when he exited, a white towel fastened enticingly low around his waist.

"Good morning," he said, flashing her a lopsided smile.

Why did she have to love the way he did that? Coming up on her elbow, she said, "Morning."

"Did I wake you? I was trying not to. You were sleeping so peacefully."

"No. The thunder."

He allowed the towel to fall, then padded across the carpeted floor, stopping in front of the mahogany-colored dresser. Even unaroused his manhood was impressive. The way it swayed back and forth with each step he'd taken derailed her train of thought.

Snatching her eyes away from his tight ass, she met Lauder's gaze across the room. A knowing smile lit his handsome face. She bit back guilty laughter. Yep, she'd been checking him out. But something told her he'd liked it.

"You're up early," she said.

He slid into a pair of dark gray fitted boxer briefs. "I have a meeting."

Climbing into bed behind her, he draped his arms over her waist and smoothed his hand up and down her stomach. Her skin prickled from his warm touch.

He kissed the nape of her neck. "I'd much rather spend this stormy Friday in bed with you."

Willow beamed. "Oh, yeah?"

"Yeah. I hate going out in this type of weather. Plus, I'm exhausted."

Not exactly the response she'd been expecting. Foolishly, she'd hoped his reluctance to leave had something to do with her. "Yeah, those are both valid reasons."

Lauder kissed her bare shoulder. "True, but my main reason for not wanting to leave is purely a selfish one."

"Really?"

"Yes. And I've never considered myself a selfish man, but I don't want to share you with the world. I want to keep you in my clutches all day."

"That's not really all that selfish. However, it could be a problem for the both of us." Lauder peppered her skin with kisses, causing her to tingle all over. *"Mmm."*

"What would be the problem?"

Drunk with desire, it took her a moment to remember her points. "You would lose potential business. I would miss my flight."

Lauder froze. "Your flight?"

"Yes. It departs at one."

"Cancel it. I'll have my assistant rebook us for Sunday."

Lauder's words sounded more like a command than a request. Still, it was tempting. Unfortunately, she had to decline. For one, she hadn't packed enough for the weekend. She'd never considered he'd want to spend the entire weekend with her. Okay, maybe it had briefly crossed her mind, but she hadn't given much weight to the idea.

For two, she'd told Hannah she would return today. Plus, there were things at the office she needed to handle. For three... *Oh, that dreaded three*. For three, feelings for Lauder that had lain dormant for years were surfacing. More time with him would only plunge her deeper. Was she prepared to risk being submerged?

Obviously, she was. This was the first time in a long while she'd even toyed with the idea of spending the weekend with a man. Especially one she wasn't committed to.

Lauder kissed her neck. "I can see you crafting an excuse in your head."

Yes, she was. They'd spent all night making love. All night in each other's arms. And now he wanted them to spend the weekend together. How could she say no?

"Okay, I'll stay." Maybe she should have held out a bit longer.

"I really want to kiss you right now," he said. "But if I do, I will never leave this room. And I really need to leave this room."

Just then, the telephone rang, startling them both.

"Dreena," he said.

While Lauder took the call, Willow escaped to the bathroom. Before exiting, she brushed her teeth and gargled with the minty-fresh mouthwash she'd packed. She wasn't going to let Lauder escape without at least a peck.

When she rejoined him in the bedroom, he'd partially dressed. Socks, dark blue tailored suit pants, a crisp steel blue shirt, partially unbuttoned. Even clothed, he tempted her.

He turned, his eyes raking over her naked body. Pulling his bottom lip between his teeth, he groaned. "You're playing dirty."

"What?" she questioned innocently. "I had to use the bathroom."

He massaged his cheek as if he were trying to decide what to do with her. "Come here."

She performed a slow, sexy stroll toward him. As she meshed against his chest, another deep rumble escaped from him. Her hands explored his pecs, teased his nipples, glided down his chest, slid over his six-pack and rested against the hardness in his pants.

She stroked him gently. "So, what did Dreena say?"

He moaned. "That the car is waiting."

"Too bad. I guess we'll have to pick up where we left off later."

It would give them both something to look forward to.

Lauder slid into the back of the town car next to Dreena. "How late are we going to be?"

She checked her rose gold timepiece. "We'll make it. Even with this treacherous weather."

"Good." He ran his hand down the front of his pants, ironing out invisible wrinkles, then blew a heavy breath.

"Rough morning?"

"Yeah. I couldn't find my other shoe."

Dreena burst out laughing. "Ah. So that's what took you so long?"

Actually, it was bending Willow over the dresser and taking her from behind that had held him up. Of course, he had no intentions of sharing that tidbit of info. Temptation was one hell of a drug. And he'd damn near OD'd.

Normally, on these types of rides, he and Dreena discussed their game plan. Not this morning. The only conversation was taking place in his head.

Lauder propped his elbow against the window and massaged the side of his face. He'd rarely ever slept with the same woman twice. Yet, he'd practically begged Willow to spend the weekend with him. He chuckled, but warned himself not to get too caught up in Willow, because none of this was real.

Ha! Who was he kidding? What he felt for Willow was as real as real could get for him. The woman was in his system. And he liked having her there.

His night with Willow had made one thing blazingly clear to him: he wanted more than just make-believe with her.

No strings.

It was what they'd agreed to.

But after last night, there were strings. And with those strings, he planned to bind her so tightly to him that she'd never want to be free.

Chapter 14

After breakfast the following morning, Lauder surprised Willow by arranging for a rental car, a black convertible with peanut butter–colored leather seats. The vehicle was perfect for the gorgeous Saturday. They spent hours exploring Memphis. Unlike the day before—when they'd remained hotel bound because of the torrential rain and occasional thunderstorms—sunny skies and a comfortable seventy-six degrees greeted them today.

Willow closed her eyes, tilted her head back and enjoyed the warm air whipping against her cheeks. For the first time in a long time, she felt so alive. Had Lauder done this to her? She glanced in his direction, a smile curling her lips when she admired him. Yep, he had.

The black ball cap he wore was pulled low, shading his eyes. Her gaze crawled across his commanding jaw, over his pronounced Adam's apple, along his solid shoulders and down his strong arms. Arms that had held her so securely during the night that she hadn't awakened once.

"You okay?" Lauder asked.

"Yes."

A short time later, they arrived at the National Civil Rights Museum. Standing in the parking lot of the Lorraine Motel, staring at the location where Martin Luther King Jr. was assassinated, overwhelmed her.

She swallowed the painful lump of emotion lodged in her throat as they entered the historic building. The tour through history affected her so much that the two-hour visit left her in tears.

Outside, Lauder pulled her to him, wrapped her in a warm embrace and held her tight. It was soothing to be inside his arms.

"Do you want to go back to the hotel?" he asked.

"No, I'm okay." She pushed away from his chest.

Lauder stared at her as if he were attempting to decide whether or not to believe her.

She smiled. "I'm good, really."

He took her word for it, and they continued their journey. Venturing to the Memphis Zoo lightened her mood. Afterward the visit to B.B. King's Blues Club on Beale Street for lunch made her entire day.

Lauder ordered the famous lip smacking ribs, while she ordered the pulled pork platter. They laughed, chatted and enjoyed the live band playing the blues.

Selfishly, Willow liked the fact that they weren't hounded by people wanting to shake Lauder's hand, talk politics or snap pictures with him. Here they were just tourists.

After lunch, they strolled hand in hand down Beale Street.

"Voodoo needs. Sounds interesting," she said, dragging Lauder into Tater Reds.

The first thing to catch her eye was the colorful skull-shaped salt-and-pepper-shaker set. And moon pies. She had to have them both.

Two hours later, they were back in the vehicle.

"I think I've eaten too much pork. My feet are swelling," she said.

Lauder's eyes left the road briefly to eye her. "I can carry you into the hotel."

She laughed. "I can manage, but thank you for the offer."

An hour or so later, Willow and Lauder relaxed on the hotel's rooftop sundeck. The gorgeous space outfitted with several sitting areas overlooked the Mississippi River. They chose one of the four L-shaped wicker-styled sofas situated under a metal canopy.

Surprisingly, they were the only ones who occupied the deck. Lauder pulled her legs into his lap, removed her now snug sandals and massaged her tired feet. This, she could get used to.

"God, that feels amazing," she said.

"Did you enjoy yourself today?"

"I haven't had that much fun since…" She searched her memory. "I don't think I've ever had that much fun. Thank you."

"No need to thank me. I needed today. My world is like an endless roller coaster right now. Today was like a leisurely merry-go-round. I enjoyed it. I need more days like this."

Silence fell between them. They stared at one another as if both were trying to read the other's thoughts.

"I don't really know you, Lauder."

Lauder's brows bunched slightly. "What do you mean?"

"I've spent the past two nights in your bed—two wonderful nights I don't regret—but I don't really know you. Not this version of you. I still have that seventeen-year-old boy who deflowered me stuck in my head." She brushed a hand down his cheek. "I want to get to know the man he's become."

Lauder's eyes left her and moved to her feet. "Okay. What do you want to know?"

"Everything. Your likes. Your dislikes. What gives you strength, courage. What scares the hell out of you. Your journey from an orphan to a freaking senatorial candidate. I want to know it all, Lauder."

When Lauder returned his gaze to Willow, he saw the sincerity in her eyes and felt something slamming into his chest. No one had ever taken the time to peel back his layers.

Willow smiled. "Too much, too soon?"

He shook his head. "No, it's not that. I'll be an open book for you."

"Then what?"

"It's n—"

"And don't tell me it's nothing, because I can see that it's something."

He sighed. "You're the first woman who's ever asked me those questions." He slid his gaze away again before she could witness how much the inquiry meant to him.

"Speaking of women," Willow said, "why are you still single?"

"I'm not single, Ms. Dawson." He lowered his voice. "I'm in a pretend relationship with a beautiful woman."

A smile twitched at Willow's lips. "Let me rephrase. Why *were* you single?" Her tone lowered. "Before this pretend relationship."

A loaded question. He could have rattled off a hundred reasons, all rooted in his inability to let anyone get too close. Instead, he said, "Guess I've never found that special one. At least, not the one I could see spending a lifetime with. Plus, I'm not the easiest man to love."

Though faint, he felt Willow's body stiffen. Had it

been from the mention of love? Did the emotion frighten her as much as it did him? Deciding not to address her reaction, he continued, "What about you? You *were* single, too."

She shrugged one shoulder. "Same as you, I guess. That special one has never found his way to me."

Until now, he wanted to say.

Another beat of silence played between them, but the descent into quiet didn't last long.

"What happened to you after you left the group home, Lauder? Where did you go?"

"The Cardinal House."

"The Cardinal House? What is that?"

"It was a ranch for wayward boys." He gave a weak chuckle. "It was probably the best thing that could have ever happened to me. I met some of my best friends— brothers—there."

"I'm glad it worked out for you."

Lauder noted a hint of sadness in Willow's eyes. "I thought about you every single day."

"I thought about you, too." Willow's lips parted as if she wanted to say more, but closed as if she reconsidered whatever lingered on her tongue. Finally, she said, "A ranch?"

"Horses, cows, chickens, pigs. If it were any creature in need of love, Momma Carlisle had them."

"Carlisle. Isn't…?"

He nodded. "Chuck's grandmother ran The Cardinal House. A spunky sixtysomething woman who didn't take shit from any of her boys. And trust me, we tried her plenty."

"So that's how you and Chuck met?"

"Yeah. He spent summers at the ranch. A pretty boy from up north. I *hated* him with a passion."

"Hated him? Why?"

"I was jealous," he said plainly. "He had the doting parents, new everything, the best grandmother in the world. I was jealous."

"Come here." Willow leaned forward and cradled his face between her hands and kissed him gently. "I get it." She pecked him again. "I still get a little jealous when I travel with Hannah to family functions. I envy not having grown up around so much love."

Lauder swiped a thumb back and forth over Willow's leg. "Is that why you want to adopt?"

"Yes. I want to give a child all the love I wish someone would have given me."

When her eyes clouded with tears, he pulled her into his lap. "Don't cry. I promise you'll never feel that kind of emptiness again."

She rested her head on his shoulder. Swiping at her cheek, she said, "How did you and Chuck become best friends if you hated him?"

"Rice Krispies Treats."

Willow laughed. "Rice Krispies Treats? Oh, this should be good."

"One night he was in the kitchen making a batch. I kept walking by the door peeping them out. I wanted one so bad my mouth watered. But I was too proud to ask."

"So what happened?"

"I guess he figured out what I was doing. He came into my room, placed a plate on my nightstand, then walked out without saying a single word. I ate the entire plate by myself."

"You do have a huge appetite."

When he pinched her thigh, she squealed.

"The next day I asked Chuck if he wanted to go fishing. The rest is history."

Lauder and Willow spent the next hour chronicling their lives for one another. He'd told her how he'd stripped for a short time to help pay his way through college—which she didn't believe. He made a mental reminder to show her some of his old moves soon. He shared with her how he'd worked part-time washing dishes on campus, tutored mathematics, graduated with a major in business and minor in accounting.

"How did you get into repurposing?"

"My first place out of college was a dump with a capital *D*, but it was cheap as dirt. The owner said I could do anything I wanted to it. I took some free classes at the local hardware store. I used what I'd learned to transform my tiny studio apartment into a masterpiece. When my landlord actually paid me to do the same to the other units, I knew I was on to something. I fell in love with breathing life back into the lifeless."

"I like that," Willow said. "Breathing life back into the lifeless."

"Look at me," he said. When she did, he said, "Thank you."

"For what?"

He kissed the palm of her hand. "For everything." Especially for making him feel again. But he kept that to himself.

"Cryptic, but you're very welcome."

Silence descended, but only for a moment.

"Do you remember suggesting The Willow Tree host a fund-raising gala for the kids?"

"Yes."

"I have someone working on it. It was a great idea. Thank you for suggesting it," he said. "Willow Dawson, will you accompany me to the gala?"

"Lauder Tolson, of course I will."

A second later, he collected her sandals and stood with her in his arms.

"Where are we going?" she asked.

"To our room."

Willow laughed. "Why? I'm enjoying it out here."

"I guarantee you'll like what I have planned for us in the room better."

"And what is that, exactly?"

"Lots of slow, tender lovemaking. What do you think about that?"

"Hmm." She shrugged. "I guess it sounds all right."

"Sounds like you need a little convincing."

Ten minutes later, Lauder had Willow naked and in the shower. He lathered a rag and washed it over her back, resisting the desire to take her right then and there.

Willow moaned. "I'm not sure which you're better at, massaging my feet or washing my back. I'll just say you're equally skilled at both?"

"I'm pretty good at a few more things, too."

"Like?"

Lauder tilted her head to the side. "Like kissing you right here." He kissed her neck. "And right here." He kissed her shoulder.

"*Mmm*. What else are you good at, Mr. Tolson?"

Something about the way she said his name, all sultry and desire laced, aroused him. He turned her swiftly and forced her back against the shower wall.

Willow gasped, then grinned. He placed his hands on her waist and crawled them up her sides. Lifting her arms, he pinned them above her head. Pushing his body against hers, he traced her lips with the tip of his tongue. She tilted her head forward in an attempt to kiss him.

He drew back. "Don't be greedy."

"But I'm hungry."

"For what?"

"For you." Her eyes lowered below his waist.

He kissed one cheek, then the other. Staring her in the eyes, he said, "What are you doing to me, woman?"

"The same thing you're doing to me, I hope."

Clearly, she thought he was referring to this moment, but he was talking about the internal effects she was having on him.

Urgently, he cradled her face and kissed her wildly. Damn, he swore her mouth got more delicious every time he tasted it. Willow met each of his impatient tongue strokes. He desperately wanted to lift her leg and thrust into her hard and raw.

The idea of making love to her without a barrier made his erection throb even more. With his breathing heavy, his heart thundering, his pulse erratic, he snatched his mouth away. "You do crazy things to me."

Shutting off the water, he hoisted her into his arms and carried her into the bedroom. The heat radiating from her core made him dizzy. He wanted her so bad his hands shook when he reached for a condom.

"Turn off the lights," she said. "I want you to feel your way around my body."

"No. I want to see your face when I enter you." There was another reason, but he wasn't ready to confess it yet. With one swift thrust, he was inside her warm wetness. Willow's mouth fell open, but nothing escaped. Not a single sound. He ran his tongue along the vein that bulged in her neck. "You feel so damn good." And he felt right at home inside her. He captured her mouth in another rough and wild kiss.

"Take me harder," she managed to say through their joined mouths.

It was a challenge he couldn't resist. Gripping the back

of the headboard, he drove into Willow with primal force. The sensation was so intense, he growled like a ferocious beast. Nearing his breaking point, he continued to deliver sturdy strokes. When Willow's muscles pulsed around him, he exploded, yelling her name over and over again.

Drained of every drop of his energy, he collapsed down onto Willow. His heart pounded in his chest. He was sure she felt it because he could feel hers. "I'll move in a second," he said against her damp skin. "I can't move right now."

Willow hugged her arms around him. "Don't move. I want to stay like this all night. I want to feel like this… forever."

Forever sounded good to him. "I love going for late-night swims when I can't sleep. I like lazy days on the couch watching reruns of *In the Heat of the Night* and *Matlock*. I love to eat. Pasta is my weakness. Specifically lasagna. I love reading biographies. I hate brussels sprouts, because I was force-fed them when I was young. I dislike people who only think about themselves. I hate—"

"Being in the dark," Willow said, finishing his thought.

He lifted his head to eye her. "Yeah, I hate the dark."

"Because of the closet event you mentioned at the seniors' function?"

"Yes."

"If I asked you for details, would you give them to me?"

Willow's expression held a great deal of compassion. "Possibly." More like definitely, because, for some reason, he always wanted to give her pieces of himself. Even the jagged ones. Hell, he'd even admitted to her to being afraid of the dark. But this was one time he didn't want to delve into his past. This moment was too beautiful to spoil with that kind of darkness.

Thankfully, he got his wish. Willow guided his head back down onto her shoulder. But now, he was curious. Lifting his head again, he said, "You're not going to ask?"

"No. Just knowing that you're willing to share something I'm sure is painful for you to talk about is enough. Plus, this moment is too beautiful to spoil."

Damn, was she in his head?

Willow continued, "Let's just enjoy it. Enjoy each other. Enjoy this weekend. And if one day you feel the need or desire to share, I'll listen. Without judgment."

"Thank you."

Things were quiet between them for a long while, each clearly lost in their own thoughts or simply enjoying the moment. Perhaps both. With Willow now snug in his arms, her head placed appropriately over his heart, there was no other place in the world he would rather be.

Chapter 15

It had been two weeks since Willow had returned from Memphis, and she was ready to go back. She couldn't get her weekend with Lauder out of her head. Every time she thought about how much time they'd spent exploring the city and exploring each other, she smiled.

Standing in an elevator full of Raleigh's finest, all she could think about was how none of them held a candle to Lauder. Her body ached for his touch. And boy, did he know how to touch her.

There had been a moment after returning to North Carolina she'd considered telling him that they should go back to the way things were prior to Memphis, prior to their no-strings agreement, because it scared her how attached she was growing to him. But she hadn't been able to bring herself to say the words.

Shaking Lauder from her thoughts, she checked her watch. The early morning meeting she'd had with the police chief had gone longer than expected. A feeling of gratitude filled her when she considered why she'd been summoned to the Raleigh Police Department headquarters. Police Chief Braun wanted to personally thank her for the work she'd done for them on a cold case. Using her skills, she'd made it possible to positively identify the skeletal remains of a young college student who'd gone missing years earlier.

Willow's facial reconstruction had given a very prominent family the closure they'd sought for over a decade. God, she loved her job. Exiting the elevator, then the building, she headed for her vehicle. She was so late for her lunch date with Hannah. The woman was probably gnawing on her arm by now.

"Willow."

The familiar voice behind her caused her to stop mid-step. Taking a second to gather her thoughts, she turned. Plastering a smile on her face, she said, "Reggie. Hey."

Being that Reggie worked in the cybercrimes division within the police department, she knew there was a good chance she'd run in to him. His silvery-gray gaze locked on to her. Probing. Assessing. For the first time ever, she felt uncomfortable around him. Something felt…off.

"Long time, no see," he said.

"Yeah, it has been. You look…good. Great, actually." No one could deny how handsome he was. Smooth caramel skin. Tall. Fit. And those eyes. She seriously doubted he'd had any trouble replacing her as a bed buddy.

"You look good, too," he said. "Happy. I guess it's the new relationship with that politician."

Reggie flashed a tight smile that almost appeared painful for him to display. "I should have called, Reggie. I—"

"A text, Willow. No explanation. Just a line that said you couldn't do us anymore. A year and a half you shared my bed, and you couldn't give me the common courtesy of ending things properly. We—" He stopped abruptly, his jaw clenching tight. "A simple call."

Talk about feeling like crap. "You're right, Reggie.

I owed you that much. Before all else, we're friends. I should—"

"*Were* friends," he corrected.

"Were?" She realized how stupid the question was the second it slipped past her lips. Why in the world would he want to continue being friends with her? She'd devalued their friendship.

Reggie laughed bitterly. "Would your man be okay with you hanging out with the dude you used to sleep with?"

Willow massaged the side of her neck. Well, when he put it like that... Reggie's hardness stunned her. He'd always been one of the most gentle men she'd known.

"I didn't think so," he continued. "Even if that wasn't an issue—" he shook his head "—I couldn't be your friend, Willow. You know how I feel about you. How I've always felt about you. Whether you choose to admit it or not."

"Reggie...you knew what this was going in. You knew there would never be anything between us. Other than sex," she said in nearly a whisper.

Reggie clapped his hands together, startling her.

"Nearly two years, Willow. We slept together for nearly two years. How could you not feel a *hint* of something for me?"

Willow hugged her arms around her body. "I'm sorry, Reggie."

He shook his head. "Are you even capable of feeling anything for someone?"

The comment took her by surprise. And angered her. *How dare*... Her arms fell to her sides, and she leveled him with her eyes. "I'm very capable of having feelings for someone. I was just never capable of having feelings for you."

With that, she turned and walked away, leaving Reggie to absorb her brutal words.

The drive to the restaurant gave her time to cool off. Once she had, she regretted how snarky she'd been to Reggie. But in her opinion, he'd earned it with such a hurtful and uncalled-for remark.

Still, she felt awful. *Maybe I should apologize.*

Fishing her phone from her bag, she dialed Reggie. Just like she'd expected, he didn't answer. Could she blame him? Choosing not to leave a message, she disconnected the call. Though she hated the way things had ended between them, it was for the best. She knew that now more than ever.

Ten minutes later, Willow sat inside the Carolina Grille recounting her interaction with Reggie to Hannah.

"I don't like saying I told you so, but I told you so," Hannah said. "I knew he was sweet on you."

"I deserve that," Willow said. She pushed her half-eaten burger away. "What if Reggie's right, Hannah? What if I've gone so long not feeling anything for a man that I'm barren inside?"

Hannah stopped midbite of a french fry. Dropping the crispy potato, she said, "Close your eyes."

"Why?"

"Just humor me and do it."

Sighing, Willow did as Hannah instructed. "Now what?"

"Just wait." A couple of seconds later, Hannah said, "Lauder Tolson."

A slow smile curled Willow's lips. A warm sensation swirled inside her stomach. Her pulse kicked up just a notch as an image of his beautiful face burned into her head.

Hannah chuckled. "Now...tell me you actually believe

you're incapable of feeling. The way you're glowing tells me you're feeling a lot. A whole lot."

Yes, she was. But she shouldn't be.

"Reggie is some kind of computer geek, right?"

Hannah's words drew Willow back to reality. *Geek* was putting it mildly. *Genius* would have been more fitting. He was so good in fact, he'd been approached by the FBI. Ultimately, he'd chosen to continue his work in cybercrimes with RPD. "Yes, he is. Why?"

"I don't want to sound paranoid, but he could easily gain access to your life. When you get home, cover your laptop camera with a sticky note. That way he can't watch you sleep or shower."

Willow gave a soft laugh. "You make him sound like some kind of unhinged ex-lover."

Hannah flashed her palms. "Hey. You never know. Better safe than sorry."

Willow considered her friend's words. *Could Reggie... Nah.* She shook Hannah's words out of her head. The whole notion was ludicrous. Besides, Reggie was too much of a gentleman to stoop to such a level. But she had to admit, she was a wee bit rattled.

Typically, the first thing on Lauder's mind when he woke was food, but the only thought inside his head since he cracked open his eyes an hour ago was Willow. He wished she was in his bed right now. His manhood stirred at the thought of sliding between her thighs.

"Down boy," he said, gripping his erection. "You'll get your dose of her soon enough."

He tossed a glance at his bedroom door as if doing so would cause her to miraculously appear, then laughed at his whimsical thinking. "This woman is driving me insane," he said, tossing his legs over the side of the bed. But he liked it.

Lifting his cell phone from the nightstand, he sent Willow a text:

Good morning, beautiful. Didn't want to call in case you were still asleep. I woke up with you on my mind. Can't wait to see you later.

He sent the message and placed the phone back down. Before he could stand, it chimed. Retrieving it, he read Willow's reply.

Good morning, handsome. Actually, you did wake me. This morning around four o'clock.

Lauder glanced at the clock. 7:17. With his curiosity piqued, he replied back with three question marks.

Willow's response came quickly.

LOL. I knew that was coming. I had a very lifelike dream about you. I woke myself up moaning your name.

A surprised face emoji, winking emoji and a fire icon followed her message. Instead of texting back, Lauder called her. When Willow answered, he said, "You should have called me. I would have made your dream a reality."

Her tone was tired when she said, "At four in the morning?"

"I'm on call for your sexual fulfillment twenty-four hours a day."

"Are you sure you want to give me that kind of access?"

He chuckled. She'd be surprised at the things he wanted to give her. "Absolutely."

Willow laughed. "Are we still on for tonight?"

"We are. And no, I'm not telling you what we're doing. Just dress comfortably. Like T-shirt, jeans and sneakers comfortable."

"A man of mystery."

They chatted a while longer. Before ending the call, Lauder informed her he'd be at her place at six to pick her up.

After a quick trip to the bathroom, Lauder slid into his jogging attire, then headed into the kitchen for something to hold him over until after his morning run with Chuck.

Deciding on a bowl of cereal, he leaned a hip against the counter and thought about Willow…again. He couldn't wait to see her. He had a fun-filled evening planned for them.

The doorbell rang, snatching him from his thoughts. With the bowl still in his hand, he sauntered toward the door, pulling it open. "What's up?"

"'Sup," Chuck said, brushing past him.

"Want something to eat?"

"Heck, no. Man, I don't know how you can eat before running and not puke everywhere."

Lauder circled a hand over his midsection. "A stomach of steel."

Retrieving a water bottle from the fridge, Chuck twisted off the top and took a long swig. Lauder laughed to himself. The man couldn't stomach food before a run but could down a trough of water.

"Did you take care of that for me?" Lauder asked, rinsing his empty bowl and placing it in the dishwasher.

"I did." Chuck leaned forward, resting his forearms on the countertop. "Refresh my memory. Didn't Willow ask you *not* to intervene?"

"She did."

"But you're doing it anyway?"

"I am."

"Yeah, that makes sense." Chuck shook his head. "So sad."

"What?"

"L, this is exactly what you do when you need an easy escape. You do something you know will piss the woman off, then you say it's not working and you slide right out of the relationship." Chuck shook his head again. "A damn shame, too. I actually liked this one."

Lauder didn't argue because Chuck was right. Typically, when things got too uncomfortable, he bounced. *Typically.* He rested his palms against the island. "Not this time, man. Trust me. Willow's..." His words trailed. "She's special. Plus, we're not in a relationship, so there's nothing to slide out of."

"How do you think she's going to respond when you tell her you did precisely what she asked you not to do?"

"Honestly, I don't see why she would have an issue with it. Is it really so bad to try to get her name bumped up the list?"

"No."

"Thank you."

"However, that's not the issue you're going to encounter. You're going against her wishes. Your intentions are grand. But we're rarely judged on good intentions, just bad outcomes."

Lauder allowed Chuck's words to sink in a moment. In his head, Willow would jump up and down with excitement and scream, "Thank you, Big Daddy," then shower him with kisses. But in actuality, she'd probably be pissed. It was a chance he was willing to take.

"I know what it's like to crave the kind of love Willow has to give to a child. There's some precious boy or girl out there right now who deserves her, needs her."

"And you?"

He sighed. "I probably don't deserve her, but I do need her, Chuckie. She makes me feel whole, complete. The last time I felt this way was twenty years ago. With Willow," he added. "She's ingrained in me, man. Fighting it feels useless."

"Aww, but that's not what I'm talking about. Are *you* ready to be a father? Which, if you're going to be with Willow, is exactly what you're signing up for. I don't want to play devil's advocate or sound like an asshole or anything, but there are a few things you need to consider."

"Like what?"

"Like how a kid will affect your political aspirations, for one."

Lauder noted the slight elevation of Chuck's tone. He knew Chuck had big plans for him. Lauder also had them for himself. But some things were more important than others. Things like love, family, a sense of a bigger purpose in life. They were all the things he thought about when he thought about Willow. "I'm ready to be anything she needs me to be, Chuck."

Chuck eyed him for a long time. "You're in love with her."

Lauder wasn't sure if it were a question or a statement, but he responded with "Honestly, I'm not sure I've ever stopped loving her."

"After all of this time?"

Lauder nodded slowly. "I know it doesn't make sense to you. Hell, it doesn't even make sense to me, but Willow makes me feel...worthy. I'm not even sure that's the right word I'm looking for. But the second I lay eyes on her, hear her voice, my world gets a little brighter."

"Yeah, you're far gone."

They laughed. When they settled, Chuck twirled his wedding band around his finger, eyeing it conspicuously.

"When are you going to take it off?" Lauder asked.

Chuck sighed. "Soon."

"It wasn't your fault, Chuck. It was Kym's decision to drink and drive."

"Yeah, but the only reason she was in that damn bar getting wasted was because I'd told her I was filing for divorce."

Lauder so desperately wanted to remind his best friend that Kym's infidelity also had been her decision, but he bit his tongue.

Chuck massaged the back of his neck. "Anyway." Coming to a full stand, he said, "We need to talk about next Friday's Meet the Press event. If Reno Patterson is there, he'll definitely be out for blood. He's a staunch Edmondson supporter."

Chuck sounded exhausted, and Lauder regretted opening up that wound. "The media talk can wait, and so can running. I'm starving. Let's get some breakfast. My treat." By the look in his eyes, Lauder was sure Chuck was about to decline. But he didn't, surprising him, because the man was usually all about business.

"I could go for a waffle, bacon, eggs, maybe some grits," Chuck said.

"Then let's do this."

"Let's."

Lauder grabbed his keys from the counter, and they headed out the door. Chuck's question lingered in the back of Lauder's head. How would Willow respond?

Chapter 16

At exactly five forty-five that evening, Lauder pulled in front of Willow's residence. The brownstone made him think of Manhattan. Outside his vehicle, his gaze slid skyward to the rooftop terrace. The view from up there was amazing. Even better with Willow in his arms.

Making his way to her front door, he rang the bell. Willow's sweet voice called out. A second later, the door opened. The moment his eyes landed on her, something knotted in his stomach. The off-the-shoulder sparkly black T-shirt she wore exposed her right shoulder. Instantly, he wanted to feather her skin with soft kisses. What really enticed him more were her shiny lips.

"Come in," she said, stepping aside. "I'll be ready in two minutes, I promise. Make yourself at home."

When she turned, his eyes lowered to her perfectly portioned ass filling out the jeans she wore so well. He licked his lips. "Can a brother get a peck, a graze of the lips, something?"

She backtracked, pressed herself against his chest and smiled. "How could I have been so thoughtless?"

Lauder pouted playfully. "I don't know, but it really hurt my feelings."

"I promise to make it up to you," she said, puckering her lips.

"I like the sound of that."

He covered her mouth with his, kissing her slow and deep. Her strawberry-flavored lip gloss lingered with him long after the kiss ended.

"I have something to show you," she said excitedly. "I wanted to wait until tonight, but... I can't."

"What is it?"

Taking his hand, she led the way to her bedroom. Oh, yeah. Anything she had to show him in there had to be good. A wicked grin spread across his face. "I love surprises."

"Close your eyes. And no peeking."

"Yes, ma'am."

With her mouth dangerously close to his, she asked, "Do you trust me?"

He didn't trust easily, but didn't hesitate saying "Yes."

She gave him a feather-soft kiss. "Good."

A second later, he heard a click and instantly felt the assault of darkness inside the room. The eagerness he felt a moment earlier faded, replaced with severe unease. His heart rate kicked up a notch, and his breathing grew unsteady. Anxiety heated his neck and rose to his ears, causing the edges of them to burn. His stomach churned, and he realized he'd subconsciously positioned his foot to flee the room.

"Okay, you can open them."

After several seconds of hesitation, he allowed his clammy hand to fall.

"What do you think?"

The scene before him rendered him speechless, which wasn't an easy task to accomplish. He took several steps closer to the bed, staggered. This was amazing. "How did you do this?"

"A few strips of LED lights, duct tape and Pinterest."

Lauder stared at the burst of blue light radiating from underneath the bed, illuminating the room.

"There are several color options: blue, green, red, white and violet. You can set them to still mode or make them flash." She pressed several buttons on the remote, giving him a demonstration.

"You did this for me?" he asked, both baffled and touched by the scene.

"Yes. Do you like it?"

Lauder pulled her into his arms and hugged her tightly. "You are incredible. I love it." He cradled her face between his hands and studied her for a moment. "Thank you. Really. You don't know how much this means to me that you would do something so thoughtful. Just for me. Thank you."

A sentimental expression lit her face. "You're welcome."

He wanted desperately to strip her out of every piece of clothing she wore and show her just how grateful he was for her considerate act, but he resisted. Instead, he settled for giving her another soul-stirring kiss. Tonight, she'd experience his full gratitude.

A short time later, they arrived at their destination, and Willow's eyes widened as she scanned the brightly lit room. "Oh, my God. I'm in heaven," she said.

After an article ran about his opponent's family-man appeal, Chuck had suggested Lauder show that he was just as down-to-earth as Edmondson. Lauder remembered how Willow used to love playing video games and took a gamble on that still being the case. Something told him it was. This was a win for them both.

"So, this is okay?" he asked.

Her eyes lighting up, she looked like a kid with unlimited access inside a candy shop. "Better than okay." She rubbed her hands together like a mad scientist.

Something told him he'd created a monster. However, an hour and a half later, Lauder realized Willow was not the monster, he was.

"Oh, no," Willow said, snagging his arm when he tried to swipe the game card through the claw machine again.

"But, but...your owl," he said. He'd spent the last half hour trying to win the bug-eyed stuffed animal. With how much he'd already spent, he could have purchased her fifty of them.

"I'll survive without it," she said, confiscating the card and sliding it into her pocket.

"One more time. I'll get it this time. I can feel it."

Willow tossed her head back in laughter. "The game is rigged. Those claws are too weak to grip anything. Plus, these types of games are programmed to only pay out ever so often." She tilted her pretty head to the side. "Though after spending so much money, you would have thought the machine would have felt sorry for you and given you a pity win."

"Oh, you've got jokes." She squealed when he wrapped his arms around her and lifted her off the floor. If anyone were there snapping pictures of them, that would have been a money shot. Placing her feet back on the ground, he wrapped his arm around her shoulders and pulled her close to him. "What do you want to eat?"

Her arms looped around his waist. "Greasy pizza, cheesy nachos, a hotdog all-the-way, cotton candy, a cinnamon sugar pretzel and...M&Ms. Peanut. I love peanut M&Ms."

"Umm...you do know if you eat all of that, we're going to spend the latter part of this evening in the ER, right?"

"Yeah, you have a point. Who needs a pretzel?"

Lauder laughed. "Come on, my little garbage disposal," he said, guiding her toward the food court. If she'd had a problem being called his, she didn't voice it.

After stuffing themselves like two piglets, Lauder and Willow left the arcade and headed back to her place. He couldn't wait to get her out of those clothes. Though he was full, his appetite for her hadn't waned one bit.

He cut his eyes to Willow, her gaze planted through the passenger-side window. Lauder was unsure about a lot of things in his life, but one thing he knew for certain, he wanted her to be in his. Now. Forever.

He squeezed her hand, drawing her attention from the passing world. When she smiled at him, his chest swelled with pride. "Did you enjoy yourself tonight?"

"I had an *amazing* time. I always enjoy myself when I'm with you. Tonight. Memphis. Especially Memphis."

"Yeah, Memphis was nice, wasn't it?" He set his attention back through the windshield. "Willow, I need to tell you something." Her grip on his hand loosened slightly as though she anticipated bad news. In that moment, he reconsidered his decision to tell her what he'd done, but ultimately decided she deserved to know. "I know you told me you didn't want my help, but I had Chuck place a call to DSS."

Willow eased her hand from his. *Damn.* Well, the fact she hadn't snatched it away had to be a good sign, right?

"Why would you do that after I asked you not to interfere, Lauder?"

Though her tone remained level, he could hear the irritation in her voice. "I thought I was doing a good thing. You deserve to be a mother."

"And so do the dozens of other women who are ahead of me. I'm sure they want to be mothers just as badly as I do."

He got her argument, but his concern wasn't with the dozens of other women. He was only concerned about her happiness.

"I'm sorry. I was simply—" He stopped, deciding against making any more excuses for what he'd done. "My intentions were good, but now I realize I over-stepped." As usual, Chuck had been right. People weren't judged on good intentions.

Willow studied him for a moment. In a compassion-filled tone, she said, "Thank you for telling me. You could have kept it to yourself. Thank you for being hon-est with me."

"Always," he said without waver.

A troubled expression spread across Willow's face, and her lips parted as if she wanted to say something. A second later, she flashed a guarded smile, then set her gaze back through the passenger-side window.

What had she wanted to say to him?

Chapter 17

For an entire week, Willow had struggled with how to tell Lauder about the child she'd miscarried. Their child. Something deep down urged her to tell him. Especially after the comment he'd made about always being honest with her. Until now, she'd simply taken the stance of *what he doesn't know won't hurt him*. Now she wasn't so sure this was the best approach.

"Are you okay? You seem distracted," Lauder said, swiping his thumb back and forth along the back of her hand.

His touch always seemed to calm her frazzled nerves. Forcing a smile, she said, "Yes. Chuck has me a little nervous about this Meet the Media event." The man had made it sound like she would be under the microscope right along with Lauder.

Lauder brought her hand to his mouth and kissed the back of it. "I can have the car turn around, and we can ditch this gig. Just say the word."

"The only word that comes to mind is *murder*, because that's exactly what Chuck would do to you if you blew off a room full of reporters."

He released a single laugh. "I would have to flee the country, wouldn't I?"

"Uh, yeah, you would."

"Would you run away with me?"

"Yeah, I would."

"I guess that means you kinda like a brother, huh?"

"Kinda like" didn't even scratch the surface of how she felt about Lauder. Something wildly insane had happened to her. Somewhere between their long talks, handholding, kissing and lovemaking, he'd worked his way into a part of her that was off-limits—her heart. All the more reason to tell him about the baby.

"You a'ight. For a politician."

Lauder flashed one of those dazzling smiles. "I'll take that."

A short time later, they arrived at the five-star Cambridge Hotel in downtown Raleigh. Chuck met them at the entrance and led them through the elaborately decorated lobby. Had she not been so on edge, Willow would have fully appreciated the exquisite interior of the hotel—marble, chandeliers, an ambience of excellence.

Moments later, she stood backstage with Chuck watching Lauder expertly interact with the media. He told a joke about politics that caused the room to erupt in laughter. The man sure knew how to work a crowd.

Instead of standing behind a podium, Lauder sat in a metal straight-back counter stool. As always, he appeared completely comfortable, one leg propped up on a rung, and his hands cupped in his lap. He pointed to one of the individuals in the crowd, and the brown-skinned woman grinned from ear to ear.

"Thank you, Mr. Tolson. Jamila Price with *Black Magic Media Online*. You recently sat down with our editor-in-chief. That interview—along with the photos you so graciously posed for—nearly crashed our site."

Laughter rumbled through the room.

"Okay," Lauder said with a grin.

"We received *hundreds* of comments and questions ranging from, 'He definitely has my vote,' to 'Is he available?' We've all seen the pictures of you with your beautiful queen, but what our audience wants to know is... is it serious?"

Lauder gave a single laugh, then turned his head to the right and locked eyes with Willow. The look of admiration in his eyes made her stomach flutter. She flashed him a soft smile, then blew him a kiss. Just for appearances, she told herself.

Still eyeing Willow, he said, "Ms. Price—" he shifted back to the woman "—you can tell your audience it is intensely serious."

The audience clapped as if his answer satisfied them in some way. Not more than it did Willow. *Intensely serious.* She liked the sound of that. Even if it had only been said to appease the audience.

"The two of you make a gorgeous couple," Jamila Price said over the thunder of applause.

"Thank—"

Lauder's expression of gratitude was cut short by someone yelling out his name.

"Mr. Tolson. Mr. Tolson."

Willow searched the crowd, her gaze landing on a husky middle-aged man.

"Damn," Chuck said under his breath.

"What's wrong?"

"Trouble."

Trouble? What kind of trouble? Willow narrowed her eyes at the man dressed in the uninspiring light gray suit, instantly disliking him, because he apparently posed some kind of threat to Lauder.

In a whisper, Chuck said, "He writes for a local conservative blog that highly favors the opponent."

"Reno Patterson with *Ticking Politics Weekly*. First, I'd like to say thank you for inviting us to delve into the most intimate parts of your life today."

Lauder gave a single nod, still appearing unfazed.

"I wholeheartedly agree with Ms. Price. You and Ms. Dawson make a striking couple." The man glanced down at his notepad. "You resided at the same foster home when you were younger, correct?"

Willow's gut told her Chuck had been right. *Trouble*.

"That's correct," Lauder said plainly.

"And you dated for a short time?"

Lauder shifted slightly in his seat, and Willow got the impression he didn't like this line of questioning. "Yes."

Reno smiled. "Would you call her your first love?"

"I would," Lauder said without hesitation.

"That's great. That's great," Reno said.

"What the hell are you up to, Reno," Chuck said more to himself than Willow. Then he went still. "Ah, shit," he mumbled a second later as if the man's motives had become clear.

Willow pressed a hand into her stomach. "What, Chuck? What is it?"

Reno pushed the brown plastic-framed glasses further up his nose. "My condolences on the child the two of you lost when you were teenagers. That must have been a traumatic experience for you both."

Willow whipped her head back toward the stage. "Oh, God," she said, slapping a hand over her mouth. The air seized in her lungs. *Oh, God*. This was not how she'd wanted Lauder to find out.

Muted chatter hummed inside the room. Panic set in. There wasn't anything she could do at the moment. She couldn't run onto the stage to explain. She couldn't smack the taste out of Reno Patterson's mouth for revealing her personal business to the world. And she couldn't dart away because her feet were planted on the wooden floor.

Though Willow could see Lauder's tightened jaw, his body language remained relaxed.

"I should go out there. He shouldn't have to face this alone."

"He'll be okay," Chuck said.

Chuck delivered the words with so much confidence she had no other choice but to believe him.

And he was right.

Despite being blindsided, Lauder addressed Reno Patterson with so much confidence that no one ever would have known that until this moment, he'd had no idea about the miscarriage.

What had started off as turmoil, Lauder quickly flipped, committing his support to teen pregnancy prevention initiatives and support for women who miscarried. He even thanked Reno Patterson for posing the question, though she had a feeling he'd, at one point, wanted to catapult out of his chair and leap off the stage onto the man.

After fielding several more questions—unrelated to the loss of their child—Lauder thanked everyone for coming out, then exited the stage. Willow took a deep breath and prepared for whatever would come.

On approach, Lauder parted his lips to say something to Chuck, but before any words escaped, Chuck flashed his palm.

"I'm already on it." Chuck strolled away with his cell phone pressed to his ear.

It was like they were telepathically connected.

When Lauder faced her, her breath quickened. Unsure

of what to say, she said the first thing that came to mind. "I'm so sorry for not—"

Lauder cradled her face and kissed her gently, pulled away slightly to stare into her tear-clouded eyes, then kissed her again. The action suggested he wasn't upset with her, but she still needed to hear it from him.

"Can I get one of those, my man," Lauder said to the passing attendant, who held a handful of the red, white and blue balloons that had decorated the space. "A white one, please."

The young man nodded and passed Lauder the string.

"One more thing," Lauder said. "Do you have an outdoor area we can utilize? Preferably some place without a lot of foot traffic."

The young man smiled as if Lauder had asked the million-dollar question. "Follow me."

Several minutes later, they were led to a secluded area after so many turns that Willow thought they'd need breadcrumbs to find their way back from the place.

Lauder removed several bills from his wallet and passed them to the appreciative man.

When they were alone, Lauder stared at her a long time in silence. She stared back, but each second that ticked past rattled her more and more. What was going through his mind? And what was up with the balloon?

"I should have been the one who told you, Lauder."

"I wish you had been."

"I wanted to. So many times." She shook her head. "It just never seemed to be the right time, so I kept putting it off."

In a tired tone, he said, "Tell me now."

Willow pushed her brows together, confused by the request. Until she realized he wanted to know what she'd gone through. Appeasing him, she spent the next several minutes giving him the morbid details.

Lauder scratched his chin. "Do you know what bothers me most about this whole situation, Willow? What really cuts deep?"

Although she was afraid to ask, she said, "What?"

"The fact that you had to go through losing our child alone. Our child," he repeated as if trying to come to terms with the notion. "I should have been there for you. I'll forever regret not being there to support you. But I'm here now, and I'm not going anywhere." Lauder reached for Willow's hand, then closed it around the string holding the floating balloon. "For Baby Tolson," he said.

Willow looked admiringly at Lauder, his eyes so filled with compassion it took her breath away. This beautiful gesture swelled her heart even more for him. As simple as it was, it touched her deeply. Swallowing the lump of emotion lodged in her throat, she said, "For Baby Tolson."

A second later, they released the balloon and watched as it floated higher and higher until it disappeared amongst the clouds.

As Willow faced him, so many emotions swirled inside her. So much happiness seeped from her because of him. Without a single doubt, she knew she loved this man.

Chapter 18

Willow couldn't get over how amazing the ballroom hosting The Willow Tree Foundation fund-raising gala looked. The huge space was decorated in a green, brown, gold and cream color scheme. Men and women dressed in black and white passed glasses of champagne and Bellinis on silver trays. It had touched her heart to walk in and see the silhouettes of dragonflies illuminating the walls. Celebrating unseen beauty, Lauder had said.

She searched for him in the crowd, to no avail. There were just too many people there. Easily three hundred. Some of North Carolina's most influential residents were in attendance, along with countless foster kids dressed in beautiful gowns and tuxedos, laughing, dancing, smiling.

Her own smile grew at the idea that this would be a memory they would carry with them for a lifetime, a memory that would hopefully serve as an indicator that someone did care.

Willow's lips parted slightly at the feel of the warm sensation flowing over her like a gentle rain. Lauder was near.

Then he appeared like a shining star in a cloudless night sky. Her heart fluttered at the sight of him, reminding her of how crazy she was about the man. And warning her that maybe it was time to pull back before she completely lost herself in him.

Lauder embraced the thud in his chest when his eyes locked with Willow's. By far, she was the most beautiful woman in the room. Despite how sexy she looked in that open-back, floor-length sapphire-colored gown she wore, he couldn't wait to peel it off her.

But first things first.

Tonight was the night. Finally, he would tell Willow he wanted more, wanted her in his life for real. No more pretending. Though their time together over the past few months had never felt forced to him. In his heart, Willow had always been his.

"Care to dance, Ms. Dawson?" he asked, extending his arm toward her.

"I would love to, Mr. Tolson."

On the dance floor, Lauder held Willow close to him, staring down into her tender eyes. In that moment, everyone else in the room disappeared, leaving only the two of them there. He got the best high on her scent, overdosed on her warmth, her energy.

"I want you," he said before even realizing the words were coming. In the middle of a dance floor was not where he'd wanted to spill his soul to her.

Willow's lips curled into a half smile. In a whisper, she said, "I want you, too, but we should probably hold off disappearing until the event's over. We don't want people talking, do we."

Honestly, he didn't give a damn what people said. "Not like that." He chuckled. "Actually, I do want you in that way, too, but I was referring to something else."

Willow stopped moving, and her expression sobered. "Something else?"

He parted his lips to explain, but decided he'd prefer what he needed to say to be said in private. Pulling her through the crowd, he dipped into what looked to be a storage closet and closed the door behind him.

The tight, dimly lit space should have freaked him out, but it didn't. That was how he knew Willow was the one. Beside her, he felt as though he could face any fear.

The scent of pine cleaner and lemon swirled around them. While it wasn't his ideal location, it would have to do.

"Lauder, what in the world is going on? Why are we—"

"No more pretending," he said, cutting her off. "I know we agreed to no strings, but I want strings. I want to be with you, Willow. A real relationship. I'm tired of pretending to be crazy about you when, in all honesty, I am."

Willow's lips parted, but nothing escaped. With the astonished look in her eyes, he wasn't sure if she were processing her response or preparing to flee.

While she decided, he continued. "I love you, Willow Dawson. I'm in love with you. I don't—"

She pressed a finger to his lips to quiet him, and he swallowed the rest of his remaining words. Had his declaration been too much for her to hear?

Willow searched his eyes as if trying to decide whether or not she should believe him. "I know how I feel about you," he said.

"So do I," she said. "I know how I feel about you. I know I love you. I know I want strings. No more—"

Before Willow could complete her thought, he cradled her face and sealed his mouth over hers. The kiss was desperate, urgent, greedy.

A few moments later, Lauder broke the kiss. "Now, I

desperately want you in that way," he said, weak with a need to be inside her.

Willow's eyes widened. "We can't… Not in here," she said. "What if someone—"

Lauder turned her in one swift motion, causing her to gasp. Guiding her against one of the metal shelves holding toiletry items, he peppered kisses against her neck, along her shoulder and down her bare back.

"Lauder," she purred softly.

Kissing his way back up, he pressed his hardness against her butt cheeks. Gliding his hand to the front of her, he teased her taut nipple through the silky fabric of the dress.

"We should…" Her words trailed, a soft moan floating from her.

At her ear, he teased her lobe with the tip of his tongue, then whispered, "Can I have you, baby? I need you so bad."

"Yes. Yes," she repeated. "I want you, too."

Lauder fished a condom from his wallet, unzipped his pants and rolled it down his throbbing erection. Under normal circumstances, he would have spent an adequate amount of time on foreplay, but his need was too urgent and their time too limited.

He bent Willow slightly, pulled her ass toward him, hiked her fancy dress over her hips, pushed her damp panties aside and entered her with one powerful thrust.

Willow's cries rang out. Unsure of exactly how private their location actually was, he covered her mouth with his hand. "Shh, baby." When her tongue peeped out and teased his fingers, he thought he would need someone to mask his sounds of pleasure.

Delivering hard, fast strokes brought Willow to an orgasm in record time. When her muscles clenched around him, it was too much to handle, causing him to experience his own intense release.

He held onto the shelving to keep from toppling over. Heavy breathing was all that could be heard inside the room.

"That...was—"

"Amazing," he said, finishing Willow's sentence.

"Better than amazing," she said.

On Willow's urging, Lauder made sure the coast was clear before they crept from the closet and made their way back into the ballroom.

Lauder spent the remainder of the evening feeling like a king. He eyed Willow. A king who now had his queen by his side.

Willow was just about to hit Print on the document she'd been working on for the past five hours when her screen flashed several times, went blue, then died. "What the..." Pushing the escape key several times yielded no results.

Out of habit, she reached for the phone to dial Reggie, but paused when she recalled the fact that calling him was not an option. It'd been a while since she'd talked to Reggie. Not since their confrontation outside the police department several months back. Though she knew it was for the best, she hated how things had ended between them.

Hannah burst into her office, panic altering her usually unfazed expression. "Every computer in the office is black. We've been hacked."

Willow chose to believe it was something less daunting, but it was the only thing that made sense. Especially since whatever was going on affected the entire network. Thankfully, Reggie had advised her a while ago to utilize an off-site backup company. If they had indeed been hacked, recovering their data shouldn't be an issue.

"This is his doing," Hannah said, pacing back and forth in front of Willow's desk.

Willow's brow furrowed. "His, who?"

"Reggie," Hannah growled.

Willow massaged her now throbbing temple. Yes, Reggie had the skills to crash their entire system, but he wasn't this malicious. "You really need to taper back on the crime television. It's really starting to make you paranoid." Willow laughed. And her, too.

Virginia, their office manager, rushed in. "I am so sorry. It looked like a legit email from our office supply company, but when I clicked on the link, everything went wonky. I've contacted IT. They're working on the issue remotely."

Virginia's chest heaved as if she couldn't get enough air.

Whew. For a moment, Willow had almost fed into Hannah's Reggie-having-something-to-do-with-this theory.

Lifting her hand, Willow said, "It's okay, Virginia. We've all been duped by emails before."

Virginia flashed a guarded smile, as if not believing Willow had let her off so easily. "I'll keep you updated." A beat later, she hurried from the room.

Hannah crossed her arms over her chest and gave Willow a narrowed-eye gaze.

Willow chuckled. "What?"

"You tell me," Hannah said, ambling slowly toward Willow's desk. "Normally, when something catastrophic like this happens, you're a tightly wound ball of nerves. You barely batted an eye."

"Can we truly label this catastrophic, Hannah? IT is

working on it. Plus, we have a backup system. It's all good."

"Okay, spill. Spill now."

Willow bit at the corner of her lip, barely able to contain the smile threatening to break through. She had to tell someone. "Close the door." When Hannah did, Willow continued. "I wasn't going to say anything because I don't want to jinx it."

Hannah lowered into the chair across from Willow. "Jinx what?" Her eyes danced with unconfined excitement.

"I have a preplacement assessment for adoption scheduled for next month. It's only one of many meetings, but it gets me one step closer to adopting." The idea of the assessment worried her. She'd gotten to this step before but hadn't been able to get any further. She prayed this time would be different.

"Willow! Oh, my God. This is huge. I might be a godmother slash auntie. I'm so excited for you. I'm so excited for us. This time will be a success. I can feel it."

Willow fell back in her seat. "God, I hope so, Hannah. But I'm still nervous. What if—"

Hannah flashed a palm. "Don't even say it. It's going to happen." She shrugged. "And if by some unfathomable chance they're too damn ignorant to see that you would make an excellent mother, you could always get Lauder to knock you up." A half second later, Hannah's eyes widened. "Oh, God, Willow, I'm sorry. I didn't mean to dredge up—"

Willow lifted her hand, pausing her frantic friend. "It's all right," she said, knowing Hannah was speaking of the miscarriage the reporter had questioned Lauder about months back. By the time Chuck had finished with

Reno Patterson, the man had contacted her personally to apologize.

It wasn't like she hadn't thought about the same thing, but they'd only been dating a few months. Asking him to knock her up at this stage in their relationship could probably be considered bad etiquette.

At five o'clock on the dot, Willow packed up her things and headed out the office door. Typically unheard of for her on a Friday, but she had plans with Lauder. About five minutes before she arrived at his place, he sent her a text stating a key had been left at the concierge desk for her, because he would be running a bit late.

She smiled when she was given the box. Her elation grew when she popped the top. Inside was the key, but also a handwritten note that said *Keep me, I'm yours*.

Entering Lauder's place without him felt awkward. And she definitely wasn't used to the little light illuminating the interior. It was usually as bright as the full day sun. Moving through the foyer, she stopped abruptly, her mouth falling open.

Rose petals and tea light candles were scattered throughout the living room. A single chair stood in the middle of the floor with a sign that read *Sit here* propped against it.

"What's going on here?" she mumbled to herself.

Before she could give it much consideration, music started to play. Easing down as directed, she waited in anticipation for what would happen next. A beat later, Lauder came into view. *Good, Lord.*

Her eyes started at the chalk-white high-top sneakers he wore and slowly crawled up his body. The sight of him in the gray jogging pants was enough alone to jostle her body from admiration to pure longing. What was it about a man in gray jogging pants that drove women so crazy?

However, this particular man had a way of working her body into a frenzy despite what he wore.

Willow gnawed at the corner of her lip as her exploring eyes raked over Lauder's bare chest. His skin glistened as if he'd been sprayed with tire shine. A black baseball cap pulled low over his head shadowed his eyes. He stood board stiff, his head low and hands locked together in front of his crotch.

When the instrumentals faded to the sound of a heartbeat, Lauder's chest pumped perfectly to the rhythm. A tune she recognized, but couldn't readily name, mixed with the beat and Lauder's entire body started to flow with it.

His movement was so fluent, so precisely timed to the melody it astonished her. Initially, she'd doubted his claims of once being a stripper. Not anymore.

He trudged toward her, pop-locking to the beat. A few feet away from her, he dropped to the floor. She gasped at the unexpected move. With one hand fixed behind him and the other bracing him in a push-up position, he ground against the hardwood floor, mimicking sizzling hot lovemaking.

There was no doubt he'd made a mint as a stripper. His biceps, forearms, back and shoulder muscles flexed with each move he made. She shifted in her seat to subdue the intensifying throb between her legs.

Maneuvering to his feet in one swift and smooth motion, Lauder stalked toward her, his eyes pinned to her as if she were prey he was about to devour. When he reached her, he positioned himself over her lap in a standing straddle.

Continuing to groove with the beat, he captured her hands and placed them against his bare chest. The feel of his hot flesh sent her body into a frenzy. Her temperature rose several degrees. If she wasn't careful, she'd suffer an anticipation-induced heatstroke.

Her nipples tightened inside her bra, becoming painful. His warm lips and tongue were the only things that could bring her relief. Eager hands roamed over his frame, appreciating every hard inch of him.

And speaking of hard inches...

With her fingertips, Willow trailed lines down Lauder's torso. Capturing one of her hands, he glided it beneath the waistband of his pants, but before she could cop a feel, he snatched it out and grinned.

She pouted playfully. "That was not n—"

Willow yelped as the chair went catapulting back. She panicked, her heart thumping against her chest, her breathing heavy. Bracing herself for the crash, she pressed her lids together tightly. Lauder caught the chair midtilt, easing it the rest of the way down.

She cracked one eye open, and the sight of Lauder's face instantly calmed her.

"I got you," he said, lowering his body until he was on top of her.

His hardness pressed into her stomach, causing fine bumps to prickle her skin. Her body hummed for him. The magnitude of her desire caused a dizzying effect.

Lauder removed his cap and flung it aside. His delicious mouth hovered inches above hers. Impatience kicked in when she considered how desperately she wanted him to kiss her, but she refused to rush this thing along. Mainly because she was receiving a great deal of pleasure from the buildup.

"Do you want me?" he asked.

"Yes."

Lauder jumped to his feet so fast it startled her. He sat on the edge of the flipped chair, bent forward and unbuttoned her pants. A beat later, he lifted her legs and removed them, along with her panties.

His eyes fixed below her waist. When he glided his tongue across his bottom lip in a slow, sexy manner, butterflies fluttered in her stomach. Unhurried, he brought his dark, hungry gaze up to meet hers. The danger lurking in his heated stare excited her.

"I want you," she said in a low, seductive tone.

His mouth curled into a wicked half smile. "I know."

After sliding down the seat of the chair, he placed one of her legs over each of his thighs. Capturing her hands, he pulled her up until she straddled his lap.

Lauder snaked a hand behind her neck and pulled her mouth close to his. "And I want you, too."

Their mouths joined in an exhilarating exchange of passion. His hands crawled down her rib cage and gripped the hem of her shirt. They broke the kiss long enough to lift the fabric over her head.

He unclasped her bra, freeing her aching breasts. Breaking off the kiss again, he sucked one of her tender nipples between his lips. She moaned with delight. Moisture pooled between her legs and she was sure the front of Lauder's pants was soaked. She wanted him inside her so badly she could barely think straight.

Dragging his tongue across to the opposite breast, he gave it equally gratifying attention. Each suckle, flick and twirl heightened her need for him. He kissed his way back to her mouth, and their lips touched. She parted hers and Lauder's tongue eased inside. He kissed her gently, thoroughly.

He broke away again and planted kisses along her jawline. "Do you believe in forever?" he asked.

She moaned when he dragged his tongue along the column of her neck. "Of course I do."

Back at her mouth again, he said, "What if I wanted to spend forever with you?"

With those words, Willow reeled back and stared at him. Did that mean what she thought it meant? Was he about to ask her to marry him?

Lauder knew he'd stunned Willow with his words by the baffled expression on her face. Heck, he'd astonished himself. He hadn't come to this decision lightly; he'd contemplated it for weeks. Each time, he'd come to the same conclusion. He wanted to spend his life with her. While he didn't know shit about being a husband, he knew with Willow he was willing to learn.

"Say something," he said.

Willow's lips parted, but nothing escaped. A second later, her lips touched his. He took that as his cue to proceed. Moving off the chair, he laid Willow back down on the carpet in front of the fireplace, kicked out of his shoes and removed his pants.

The monumental decision to propose should have given him pause, but no hesitation lingered. The idea of vowing forever to her both thrilled and terrified him. *A husband.* He'd never even had the desire to get married before Willow. He could write a book about things he'd never considered prior to Willow. "Before Willow" would be the perfect title.

An image of a swollen-bellied Willow flashed in his head. A skin-prickling sensation coursed through him. It was the most exhilarating feeling ever, and it traveled to his soul.

"Are you okay?" Willow asked.

Refocusing, Lauder said, "Perfect. Absolutely perfect."

He lowered to kiss her, but she stopped him. Directing him down on the carpet, she straddled his lap.

"You want to be in control, huh?" he asked.

Willow leaned forward and kissed him, lifted her hips and slid effortlessly down his shaft. They both released a deep, guttural moan. She worked her hips up and down, in a circular motion. He thought he'd lose his mind over how good this felt.

His hands slid down her body and kneaded her ass. "You feel so good," he said, against their joined mouths. "So damn good." Willow ground even harder against him and his head involuntarily tilted back. "Shit."

Grabbing a fistful of Willow's hair, he tilted her head back, licked a line up the column of her neck, then suckled her chin. In a swift motion, he had her on her back again. Blindly moving, he pinned her knees to her chest and drove in and out of her in swift, hard strokes.

Willow's cries tore through the room, forcing him to increase his thrust power. Beads of sweat formed along his hairline, and his heart pounded against his rib cage. His breathing grew ragged, and he swore the sparks firing through him would short-circuit his system.

"Lauder! Oh, my—"

Willow's words seized. Her mouth gaped wide open, but she didn't make a sound. A second later, she pulsed around him. The sensation triggered something inside him, and a second later, he exploded.

When he'd been milked of every drop he had to give, Lauder collapsed down next to Willow. For the next few moments, all that could be heard were the sounds of their heavy breathing and the crackle of the fire.

Easing his head to her shoulder, he said, "I'm a changed man, Willow. Don't ask me to explain it because I can't. I just know something about me feels different. I find myself wanting things that never enticed me before."

"Things like what?"

"Like a house in the country, a huge backyard, an army of kids."

"I see. And how do you plan to come about this brigade of children?"

"Adoption. But also by my wife. Hopefully, one day I'll meet a woman who I fall insanely in love with. One who I'd jump at the opportunity to call my wife. One who will be honored to have me as her husband. A woman who will be my forever. You know anyone like that?"

Lauder felt Willow's body tense ever so slightly. He didn't bother speculating why. He knew. He'd stunned her yet again.

Coming up on his elbow again, he continued, "Well, do you know a woman like that? If so, I'd love to meet her. I'd love to spend my life with her."

A sentimental expression played on Willow's face. "I—"

Before she could finish her thought, thunderous banging sounded at the front door.

"What the hell…" Lauder said, coming to his feet and yanking on his pants. "Stay right there," he told Willow, who was almost fully dressed by the time he'd gotten his pants on.

She nodded, a look of concern in her eyes. Whoever was on the opposite side of that door was going to be sorry. One for startling his lady. And two, for interrupting a special moment.

Lauder didn't bother checking the peephole. Instead, he swung the door open with force, ready to lay into whoever was disturbing them. Chuck darted past him like he was on fire and looking to be extinguished.

"Why the hell aren't you answering your phone?" Chuck said in lieu of a proper greeting.

"I was a little busy. Why the hell are you banging on my door like you're the police?"

Chuck's jaw clenched. He took a deep breath and dragged his hand over the top of his head. From that move alone, Lauder knew whatever it was…it wasn't good.

Lauder closed the distance between them. "What is it, Chuck?"

"The email—" He stopped abruptly, pressed his eyes together and groaned like a furious beast. "The computers were hacked."

Lauder arched a brow. "Okay. So, is someone working on them?" The look of defeat on Chuck's face told Lauder there was more.

"The email exchange about hiring someone to pose as your significant other was leaked. It's all over television and social media. Several news outlets are already staking out in front of the building."

Lauder's entire mood shifted. The elation he'd felt just moments before turned to outrage. "Was this Edmondson?"

"I can't say for certain, but I wouldn't put it past him. My people are working on pinpointing the source of the leak. We'll know something soon."

Lauder closed his eyes and massaged his now throbbing temples. "How bad is it, Chuck?" He didn't have to add *and don't sugarcoat it* because that wasn't his best friend's style.

Chuck sighed heavily. "Well, it's not great. We can expect some major blowback. I can spin it, but you're going to take a hit, L. Possibly a fatal one."

Lauder massaged the side of his face, unsure of what to say. They'd worked too hard on the campaign to have it go up in flames like this.

"L, I hate to tell you this, but Willow's going to feel the heat, too. Guilty by association."

The idea of Willow getting backlash for something he'd conspired to do ate him up inside. The thought of anyone hurting her filled him with savageness. "How do we protect her?"

Chuck shook his head. "We can't. All we can do is prepare her. They're going to come at her hard. The plus side, she's strong. I think she can handle it."

Lauder massaged the tightness in his neck. Edmondson would pay for this. He'd make sure of it if it was the last thing he did. "I should go tell her what's going on."

"I heard."

Both Lauder and Chuck turned toward the sound of Willow's reserved voice. Her expression held a hint of concern, but her body language was relaxed. Lauder expected her to fly off on a tangent, which would have been well within her rights, but instead, she flashed him a lazy smile. The gesture helped to soothe him.

"Hey, Chuck," she said.

"Hey, Willow."

"Chuck, my computers at the office were affected by some type of malware. My IT company says everything is fine now, but should I be concerned that the two are in some way connected?"

"No. You weren't the target here." Chuck sent his gaze toward Lauder. "I'll give you two some privacy. I'll keep you updated. No talking to any reporters just yet. Either of you."

"Okay. Thanks, man."

The two men exchanged manly hugs, then Chuck left.

After securing the door, Lauder closed the distance between him and Willow. "I'm sorry about this, baby. I never meant—"

Willow placed her index finger over Lauder's lips, quieting him. "We'll get through this. We're a team."

That was all he needed to hear. He wrapped her in his arms and held her tight. "Yes, we are. I love you."

Willow rested her head against him. "I love you, too."

The proposal would have to wait. The only thing he could think about right now, his main focus, was protecting the woman he loved.

Chapter 19

Willow had prepared to receive some backlash from Lauder's leaked emails, but had no idea it would become this taxing. Like Chuck had stated, she was considered guilty by association. She'd been called everything from an opportunist to a social climber to a disgrace to women everywhere.

Many came to her defense stating she was a victim in the situation, that she probably had no idea she was being used as a pawn in a political game. However, most of the commenters who'd appeared to be on her side punctuated their comments with something along the lines of *but she's a fool to stay with him*.

And when her desire to adopt been made public, the mob had come after her even harder. She'd been accused of using Lauder's status to unfairly influence the system. It had been said someone like her—a lying manipulator—wasn't fit to be a mother.

On several occasions, she'd wanted to come to Lauder's defense—as he'd come to hers by hiring a bodyguard to escort her whenever she ventured out—and respond to some of the nasty comments, but had resisted per Chuck's instruction.

Tossing her iPad aside, she nestled into the covers. For

the first time in a long time, she was playing hooky from work. She needed some peace and quiet. Every time she turned around, there was a reporter phoning, emailing, even contacting her through social media for a comment. This excluded the ones who'd camped out in front of her house and outside her office.

Willow closed her eyes and massaged two fingers up and down the center of her forehead in hopes of alleviating the pain she'd experienced there since this debacle had started several days ago.

As tough as she had it, Lauder was the one truly suffering. He'd taken a serious dip in the polls, falling behind the once-lagging Edmondson. It was already being reported that there was no way he could recover from this "damning scandal."

Though Chuck hadn't discovered the source of the hack, the way Edmondson had gloated when responding to questions about the situation, she was convinced the man was guilty as hell.

Bastard.

She considered what Lauder must have been going through. He'd wanted to issue a statement letting everyone know that there was nothing fake, false, pretend— and a hundred other labels that had been attached to their relationship—about how they felt about one another, which seemed like the logical thing to do. Unfortunately, Chuck had nixed it, stating something about it being bad timing. Lauder hadn't argued, but she kind of wished he had.

One thought brought her a minute amount of peace…it couldn't get any worse than it already was. Willow closed her eyes and welcomed the solitude. Before she could drift off to la-la land, her cell phone vibrated against the nightstand.

Her first notion was to ignore it but she had a change of heart when she considered it could be Lauder needing to talk. She was determined to stand right by his side through all of this. That was what women did for the men they loved.

Instead of Lauder's name flashing across her screen, it was the number for the social worker who'd scheduled her upcoming preplacement assessment. Sitting up in bed, she swiped a finger across the screen to make the call active, a smile curling her lips. She could use some good news.

"Hello?"

It wasn't long before Willow's curled lips melted into a frown. Every word Ms. Garland spoke crushed her more and more. It was all she could do to keep from sobbing into the phone. The condensed version was that her preplacement assessment appointment had been canceled, indefinitely. "We'll revisit it again when the circumstances surrounding this scandal have calmed down," the unyielding woman had said.

Not again. Willow's heart shattered into a thousand pieces.

As soon as she ended the call, her phone rang again. This time it was Lauder. Her finger hovered over the screen but allowed the call to go to voice mail. She wouldn't be any good to him now, not when she could barely process her own thoughts.

Tossing the phone aside, she cried herself to sleep.

Lauder propped himself against the floor-to-ceiling glass inside the conference room, folded his arms across his chest, crossed his legs at the ankles and fixed his gaze out the window. He should have been listening to Dreena conduct her first solo staff meeting, but his mind was far detached from the room.

The past couple of days had been sheer hell. It wasn't so much that his constituents, the media and basically anyone else with a heartbeat were ripping him to shreds; it was the fact Willow had been caught smack-dab in the center of his firestorm.

Doing something he never did in meetings, he whipped his cell phone from his pocket and attempted to reach her again. The line rang several times before the call rolled into voice mail, just as the previous five unanswered calls had.

Unable to focus on anything else around him, he left the room, then the building and headed to Willow's. The sky was a gloomy gray-blue color and it looked as if it could rain at any minute.

A short time later, he arrived at her place. Using the key she'd given him, he let himself inside. There was no sign of her on the lower level, so he climbed the stairs and headed into the bedroom.

The sight of Willow curled in bed, fast asleep, filled him with relief. He kicked out of his shoes and nestled into bed behind her. Surprisingly, she didn't flinch a muscle.

"I'm so sorry that I got you into this mess, baby," Lauder said into the back of her head. "My job is to always protect you, not place you in harm's way. I failed. Please don't give up on me."

Several hours later, Lauder woke to empty arms. Green light spilled from underneath the bed, lighting the room, also cuing him to it being nighttime. He tossed a glance at his watch. 9:27.

He'd slept damn near five hours. How was that possible? It probably had something to do with the fact he hadn't slept much over the past few days. Willow's bed had obviously supplied the safe haven he'd needed.

How had she escaped his arms without waking him? Why hadn't she woken him?

Climbing out of bed, he headed downstairs. Willow sat at the kitchen table sipping from a mug. Green tea, if he knew her like he thought he knew her.

He bent and kissed the top of her head. "Hey, baby." When he finally met her gaze, his heart skipped several beats. Her usually bright, happy eyes were bloodshot and sad. He pulled a chair close to her and eased down. "What's wrong?" He really didn't need to ask. This thing was taking a toll on her.

Willow glanced away, tears streaming from her eyes. She shook her head several times and stood. "Nothing."

He trailed her over to the sink. "Talk to me, Willow. Don't shut me out."

She leaned against the counter and lowered her head. "I got a call from Ms. Garland today."

He knew Ms. Garland was the one tasked with conducting Willow's preassessment for adoption. Receiving a call from her told him the situation was critical. "What did she say?"

"In so many words, until this scandal blows over I won't be considered for adoption."

Lauder rested his hands on her waist and rotated her to face him. "Tell me what to do."

"You've done enough, Lauder." She pushed his hands away and stalked off.

Lauder stood stunned for a second or two. Once he jolted out of the stupor, he followed her into the living room. "You blame me?" And could he really fault her if she did?

Willow whipped toward him. "Yes! I blame you. I

blame myself. I blame Chuck. I blame Edmondson. I blame the media. I blame all the people trying to make me out to be some kind of monster."

When she burst into tears, Lauder secured her in his arms and held her trembling body tightly to his chest. He'd never felt so damn powerless in his life. It killed him to know he couldn't simply make everything okay again.

Willow cried into his chest for what seemed like an eternity. Nothing he could have said would have eased her suffering, so he remained quiet, but held her close so that she at least knew he was there for her.

"I need some space, Lauder," Willow said, pushing away from his chest and freeing herself from his arms. She never made eye contact when she added, "Some time to sort my thoughts. Time away from all of this."

Lauder wanted to protest, wanted to pitch a fit. But by the look in her eyes, he knew it would have only made things worse. Defeated, he said, "Okay." Instead of arguing, he neared her, kissed her forehead, said, "I love you."

When Willow said nothing in return, it ripped him to shreds inside. He eyed her for another second, then turned and walked away.

Chapter 20

For the past half hour, Willow had worked the same mound of clay. The punching, tearing and pulling apart should have taken her mind off Lauder. It hadn't.

Resting, she thought about him.

Active, she thought about him.

Happy or sad, she thought about him.

Not that she'd had many happy days over the past week, which was how long it had been since she'd seen or talked to Lauder. She had no one to blame but herself. She'd pushed him away.

Why had she allowed her emotions to get the best of her? To blame Lauder had been unfair. To push him away had been selfish. She'd only thought about herself, how this thing was affecting her. He was affected, too. But instead of being the rock he needed—the rock he'd been for her—she'd flaked.

"You want to talk about it?" Hannah asked from across the room.

"No." A second later, she said, "Yes." Once Hannah had closed the distance between them, Willow continued, "Have you ever made a mistake you regretted the second you made it but for whatever reason you didn't correct it immediately?"

Hannah chuckled. "Uh, yeah. Mistake making is the story of my life. But it's never too late to right a wrong."

Willow wasn't so sure about that. The look she'd witnessed on Lauder's face when she'd pushed him away, the sadness in his eyes, haunted her. *Pure hurt.* And she'd allowed him to walk away. "It may be too late, Hannah. I broke something in Lauder. I saw it in his eyes." Willow's own eyes clouded with tears. "I was supposed to stand by him. Instead, I pushed him away. I have no idea why. Anger. Fear. Stupidity. Maybe a mixture of all three."

"You only asked for space, Will. Time to think. You didn't break things off. Call him."

She wanted to call him. Had wanted to hours after he'd left her place. But she hadn't. "I'm afraid."

Hannah's face contorted into a ball of confusion. "Afraid? Of what?"

"Afraid that if I call him, he'll shut me out the same way I've done to him."

"If I don't know anything else in this world, Will, I know that Lauder Tolson is crazy about you. And you are crazy about him. Trust the power of love."

Hannah was right. Willow needed to trust that what she and Lauder shared was stronger than a hasty misjudgment she'd made. Standing, Willow untied her apron, feeling more alive than she had in days. "I have to make this right."

"Go get your man, girl."

Willow rushed into her office, grabbed her purse and snatched up her cell phone. An indicator light flashed on the device, alerting her to a missed call. A smile played at her lips, believing it had been Lauder who'd called her. When she checked the missed-call log, her happiness morphed to confusion.

Reggie?

Why would he be contacting her? Especially after all of this time. She seriously doubted the timing was a coincidence. No doubt his call had something to do with this fiasco. But what could Reggie possibly have to say to her?

Maybe he was calling to sympathize with her. Or gloat on her misfortune. It really could go either way. The one thing she was certain of…getting to Lauder was far more important than chatting it up with Reggie.

Just as the thought materialized, her phone vibrated in her hand, Reggie's name filling the screen. She debated a second about whether or not to take the call. Deciding she could spare two minutes of her life, she swiped her thumb across the screen to make the call active.

"Hello."

A brief pause played on the line as if Reggie had been stunned silent by the fact she'd answered. Despite what he might have thought, she harbored no ill will toward him and hoped he felt the same way toward her.

After another second or two, Reggie spoke. "Hey."

Well, his tone didn't sound cold and calculating. Not like it had when they'd stood outside the police department. Maybe the call would be a pleasant one. "Hey," she said.

"How are you?"

Was that a trick question? "Honestly, I've been better." "I bet."

A beat of silence played over the line. Apparently, Reggie was attempting to figure out what to say to her next. Unfortunately, she didn't have time for him to muddle through his thoughts. She was on a mission. "Reggie—"

"How does it feel, Willow?"

Genuinely confused, she said, "How…does what feel?"

"Having your entire life disrupted because of someone else's selfish act."

Willow's entire body went stiff, and her mouth fell open. A cautious hand rested on her chest. Her stomach fluttered and knotted. What she was thinking couldn't be possible. Couldn't be. "Reggie..." Her words caught in her throat. "Reggie, did you do this? Are you the one who leaked the emails?"

The mere thought made Willow's head spin.

For several moments, there was dead silence on the opposite line.

"Reggie, did you do this?"

"Goodbye, Willow."

A second later, the line went dead. Willow's purse slid from her hand and fell to the floor with a *thunk*. Her cell phone followed. This was Reggie's doing. Stumbling to the nearest chair, she dropped down, the world spinning around her. She'd blamed Lauder, but this was because of her. All of this was because of her. She'd made Lauder a target. She'd cost him the election.

How could she go to him now? He would never forgive her for this.

When Lauder finally made it home a little after eleven that night, he fell face-first onto the bed, completely exhausted. Thank God tomorrow was Saturday, and he would get to sleep in. For the past week and a half, he'd worked tirelessly to get his campaign back on track. If that was even possible at this point.

Many thought he was beating a dead horse, including some in his own camp, but he planned to see this thing through to the end. Whatever the end might hold. He'd never been a quitter; it made no sense to become one now.

The most exhausting part of the interviews he'd done wasn't the probing questions about the emails, it was fielding the same question over and over again: Where was Willow?

Chuck had crafted the perfect response to the question—something along the lines of Lauder choosing to protect her as opposed to subjecting her to the constant media scrutiny. For the most part, they seemed to have bought the cover story, even commending him for shielding her.

He replayed the look on Willow's face when she'd told him about the call she received from Ms. Garland. It ate him up inside to know this situation had cost her so much.

Suddenly, he wasn't so tired after all. His distress fueled a burst of energy. Sitting up, he rested his elbows on his thighs and lowered his head. Of all the people in his life, he never had imagined that Willow would have been the one to abandon him.

He scrubbed both hands over his head. When things got rough, she'd shunned him. He'd needed her, and she'd turned her back on him. He never would have done that to her. Never. With all his might, he wanted to pretend he wasn't hurting. But he was. He was hurting like hell. But what could he do but give her what she'd asked for?

"If space is what she wants, space is what she'll get."

Pushing to a full stand, he ambled to his dresser and removed his swim trunks. He needed to clear his mind. Swimming always helped with that.

To his surprise, he wasn't alone at the lap pool. A young woman sliced through the water like an Olympian. It was quite impressive. When she came up for air, his presence apparently startled her, because she sucked in water and coughed ferociously.

Despite watching her shark-like maneuvering just moments ago, she seemed to be in distress, so he jumped in to help her. "Are you okay?" he asked after making his way to her.

Clearly unable to speak, she nodded clumsily. Finally recovering, she laughed. "I wasn't expecting to see anyone standing there. You startled me."

"I apologize. I'm usually the only one here at this hour. I'll let you get back to your workout."

"Thanks for coming to my rescue." She stuck out her thin hand. "Darcy, by the way."

"Lauder," he said, accepting her outstretched arm. "And you're welcome."

"I know who you are. That's what took me by surprise. For the record, I still plan to vote for you. Edmondson is not fit to hold office."

Well, according to the media, he wasn't, either. Curious, Lauder said, "You're voting for me even after everything that's been said about me recently?"

"I like to form my own opinions about people. Plus, I've seen the way you and Ms. Dawson look at each other. You can't fake that."

He nodded slowly. "Thank you. Now if you can convince, I don't know, several thousand of your friends to vote for me, too, that would be great."

"Done."

"You're a rock star, Darcy."

Lauder swam several lanes over to give Darcy her privacy and to secure some of his own. Despite nearly drowning when he was younger after jumping into the deep end of the pool, he'd always loved water. Taking a part-time job as a lifeguard in college had given him a greater respect for it.

After swimming the equivalent of a mile—approximately thirty-three laps—he got out. Darcy stood on the side drying off. He'd been so in his zone that he'd forgotten she was even there.

"You're pretty fast. We'll have to race sometime," she said.

Lauder slid into his pool shoes. "I'm always up for a challenge," he said. "But you're going to want to practice a little more if you plan to beat me."

Darcy laughed. "Handsome and cocky."

"And super exhausted," he said. "Enjoy the rest of your night, Darcy."

"You, too, Lauder."

A beat later he headed home. Alone. Yeah, Willow had changed him.

Chapter 21

Willow's first thought when she opened her front door at seven o'clock Saturday morning to see Chuck standing on the opposite side was that something had happened to Lauder. Her stomach knotted at the idea and panic set in. "What's wrong?"

"May I come in?" Chuck asked, his facial expression revealing nothing.

She stepped aside and allowed him entry. "Chuck, is everything okay? Is Lauder okay?"

"He's fine," he said with his back still to her.

Willow blew a sigh of relief. But if Lauder was okay, why was Chuck here?

Chuck casually perused his surroundings before turning and settling his attention on her. To say this man was intimidating would have been an understatement. His hard stare could scare a crooked man straight. That unyielding facial expression had the ability to tame a wild beast.

"Lauder needs you, Willow. Now more than ever. Your absence from the campaign trail, while understandable to some, is casting doubt with others. You should be by his side, not—"

"I think I'm responsible for this, Chuck. All of it."

When she blinked, a tear inadvertently slid down her cheek. Chuck's expression softened. Not much, but some. Whatever thoughts raced through that guarded mind of his he didn't share them with her.

"And once he finds out, he's going to hate me," she said more to herself than Chuck. "I've cost him everything. I've been trying to build up the courage to tell Lauder that this, all of this, is my fault. That Reggie is responsible for the leaked files." Her voice cracked, and she blinked back the tears burning her eyes.

Chuck blew a heavy breath, and his rigid posture relaxed. "This is not your fault, Willow. And your friend had nothing to do with it. Edmondson was behind this."

"Edmondson?" she said. "Are you sure?"

"A hundred percent. We received credible information concerning his involvement. He hired someone to dig up dirt on Lauder."

If this wasn't Reggie, why hadn't he simply said he was innocent when she'd accused him? Then it dawned on her. Because he'd probably figured she, of all people, should have known him better.

Without another word, Chuck headed for the door, but stopped shy of opening it.

Over his shoulder, he said, "He's a different man since you came into his life. A better man. A happier man. He loves you, and he deserves you. But he deserves the version of you that won't up and leave him when times get rough."

Chuck's shoulders slumped as if he regretted what he'd just said. Instead of making amends, he straightened himself and walked out the door. Willow didn't take offense at his words, because he was right. Lauder deserved far more than what she'd given him. They needed to talk.

It had taken all day, but Willow finally conjured

enough nerve to drive to Lauder's place. Both his ve-
hicles were in the underground garage, so chances were
good that he was home. Parking in a visitor spot, she hesi-
tated a moment before shutting the engine off.

She was taking a risk showing up unannounced. What
if he didn't want to see her? What if he turned her away
at the door? What if— *Stop it, Willow. You're doing this.
You have to. Or lose the man you love.* That wasn't an
option.

The pep talk worked, or more so the idea of losing
Lauder…again. Pushing all the negative thoughts and
what-ifs away, she exited her vehicle and made her way
into the building.

Willow gnawed at her lip as she waited for the elevator to reach Lauder's floor. When the doors opened,
she took a deep replenishing breath before stepping out.
Here goes nothing. Instead of using the key Lauder had
given her, she rang the bell, then knocked when there
was no answer.

After a moment of debate, she fished the key from her
purse and let herself inside. "Hello?" she called from the
foyer. Nothing. She checked the bedroom, which was
empty, too. Maybe he'd gone out with Chuck.

Only one way to find out.

Digging for her cell phone, she removed it and called
Lauder's. She pulled the device from her ear when she
heard vibrating. Following the sound into the kitchen,
she spotted his phone, next to his wallet, on the counter.
He wouldn't have gone far without both these things.

The pool.

Willow heard laughter as she neared the indoor pool
area. A woman's laugh. She pushed through the door and
went still when she saw Lauder and another woman bob-
bing together in the water, her hand in Lauder's.

What was going on?

Willow didn't hang around to find out. Changing her mind about approaching Lauder, she made a motion to slide out as quietly as she'd slid in. Unfortunately, the young woman spotted her. Maybe it was the quizzical expression on her face that prompted Lauder to turn.

Their gazes collided and held for what seemed like an eternity. Unable to hold the draining link a second longer, Willow backed away, then hurried from the room.

Rushing down the hall, she felt sick to her stomach. When it felt as if she couldn't get enough air, she stopped a moment. *Just keep moving*, she willed herself. But she couldn't. Bracing a hand against the wall, she closed her eyes to subdue her lightheadedness the shock of seeing Lauder with another woman had brought on.

"Willow?"

Lauder's voice jarred her. Without acknowledging him—and barely able to walk a straight line—she took off down the hall again. She just needed to get away.

"Willow, stop."

Finally reaching her destination, she stabbed at the down button. *Hurry up*.

"So, what…you're just going to keep running?" Lauder said.

Willow whipped her head toward him. A huge mistake. With her equilibrium already compromised, the action caused her to wobble and nearly lose her balance. Lauder rested his hands on her waist to study her. And for a brief moment, she allowed herself to enjoy his touch. A touch she hadn't felt in far too long.

"Are you okay?" Lauder asked, his tone filled with compassion.

Even though she wanted to ignore it, she appreciated the concern in his tone. Pushing his hands away, she stared at him. Her eyes lowered to his bare chest. The idea of the mystery woman running her fingers over his damp flesh, touching him, arousing him, caused another wave of nausea.

Luckily, the elevator doors opened and she attempted to make a getaway, but Lauder's solid frame blocked her escape. They eyed each other for a long time. So many emotions raged inside her that she couldn't simply focus on one. She wanted to cry, scream and run all at the same time.

"How could you?" she finally said, her tone low and filled with hurt. There was so much more she wanted to say, but nothing else would come.

Lauder's brow furrowed as if the question confused him. His jaw clenched, then relaxed.

In a reserved tone, he said, "How could I? How could you, Willow? I haven't seen nor heard from you in two weeks. *Two—*" He paused and looked away, his jaw tightening again. Eyeing her again, he continued, "I get that you're going through something. But guess what, so am I."

"Yeah, well, you seem to be getting through it A-okay."

If the statement had any effect on him, he didn't show it.

"One call, Willow. Just one text from you to at least let me know you cared would have made all the difference in the world. Nothing. Where were you? The woman who claimed to love me. Where were you, huh? Nowhere to be found."

Lauder backed away, turned and headed back toward the pool. He stopped midstride as if he were having second thoughts about leaving, but a beat later, he continued away.

Her lips parted to tell him why she'd stayed away. Why she'd been so afraid to reach out to him. Because she'd thought she was responsible for all of this. But she couldn't. Instead, she let him leave and attempted to convince herself it was for the best.

After driving around aimlessly for hours, Willow found herself at Hannah's front door at close to midnight. She rang the doorbell and waited. When there was no answer, she rang it again. The door finally opened.

"Willow?" Concern spread across Hannah's face. "What's wrong?"

Willow combed her fingers through her hair. "I—" She paused when her voice cracked. "I could really use a friend right now."

Hannah wrapped an arm around Willow and led her inside.

Drained, Willow collapsed down on the sofa, kicked off her shoes and drew her legs to her chest. "I'm sorry. I shouldn't have just shown up like this, but..." Her words trailed off as a painful lump settled in her throat.

"Don't apologize. Just tell me what's going on."

For the next hour, Willow gave Hannah the rundown of everything that had happened that day, starting with the visit from Chuck and ending with seeing Lauder in the pool with that woman and how they'd been holding hands.

"He was so angry with me, so cold. He hates me."

She had a feeling she'd lost him.

Even with the election being tomorrow, Lauder couldn't think about anything but Willow. Their encounter at the pool the past weekend still haunted him. He'd been so cruel to her. He shook his head at his actions. To add to his anguish, he'd allowed her to believe that he and Darcy had been at the pool together.

Although it may have looked suspicious, that hadn't been the case. He'd been there alone. Darcy had shown up, startling him as he'd done to her their first encounter at the pool several weeks back.

They'd raced; he'd won; she'd accused him of cheating; she'd splashed him with water; he'd splashed her back. All good-humored and innocent fun. Then they'd given each other a high five for good sportsmanship. Absolutely nothing more.

Besides, Darcy knew he was a committed man. She'd even commented on it the first time they'd met. *All innocent*, he said to himself. In fact, after he'd walked away from Willow at the elevator, he'd returned to the pool, collected his things, gone home—alone—and sulked.

"I need to tell you something," Chuck said from the small round conference table across the room. "Are you with me?"

Lauder swiveled in his chair to face Chuck. "Yeah, I'm with you."

Apparently, Lauder hadn't sounded too convincing, because Chuck sighed heavily, stood and took a seat in one of the chairs directly across from Lauder's desk.

"Look, I need you focused, L. Especially today. Just call her, man. Honestly, watching you mope around like a child who's lost his favorite teddy bear is depressing as hell."

Lauder fell back in his chair, placed an elbow on the armrest, closed his eyes and massaged his forehead. "She doesn't want to hear from me. I messed up, Chuck."

"Oh, hell. What did you do?"

"It's what I didn't do that's the problem." He eyed Chuck. "Willow came by my place on Saturday."

"Damn, L. Please don't tell me you had another woman there."

Clearly, Chuck thought he'd reverted back to the old Lauder Tolson. The one who would have simply gotten over one woman with another. That wasn't the case. A harem of women couldn't make him forget Willow.

Lauder shook his head. "I haven't thought about or wanted another woman since Willow came back into my life," he clarified. "I was at the pool. One of my neighbors was there, too. Darcy," he said as if it mattered.

Chuck sat back in his chair and crossed an ankle over his leg. "Darcy?"

Lauder nodded. "Willow jumped to conclusions and assumed we were there together. We weren't," he added for emphasis.

"You didn't set it straight?"

"No. Honestly—selfishly—I wanted her to feel what I've been feeling. Hurt. Betrayed. Thrown away." Lauder sighed. "I acted without thinking. I let my ego and pride get the best of me. Anyway... It's over. If I hadn't lost her before, I have now. At this point, there's no way she would believe there was nothing going on between me and Darcy."

Chuck pinched the bridge of his nose as though he was feeling some of the anguish Lauder was experiencing. Something caught Lauder's eyes. The absence of Chuck's wedding band.

The missing jewelry gave Lauder a little joy. It meant his friend was finally moving forward, which was a great thing. Chuck—though a little hard around the edges—was a good brother who deserved to find true happiness. Happiness like he'd known with Willow.

Pushing Willow from his thoughts, he said, "What's up with that?"

When Chuck glanced up, Lauder wiggled his ring finger.

Chuck massage his bare finger. "It was time."

Lauder didn't push Chuck beyond that explanation. A beat of silence played between them, as both men were clearly lost in their own thoughts. Silence normally soothed Lauder. Not any longer. Now the stillness only brought memories of Willow that invaded and tortured him.

"I have you to thank," Chuck said.

Lauder refocused on his friend. "Me? Why?"

Chuck leaned forward, resting his elbows on his thighs. Studying his fingers, he said, "Believe it or not, seeing how happy Willow made you gave me hope. I'd never seen you more content than when you were with her. That woman prompted change in you, bro. Good change." He shrugged.

Lauder smiled. "I think I like this tender side of you. You should show it more often."

Chuck tossed one of the VOTE TOLSON buttons at Lauder. "Don't count on it."

They shared a much-needed bout of laughter.

Sobering, Chuck leaned back in the chair. "Tomorrow's the big day. You ready?"

"What, ready to have my ass handed to me by that bastard Edmondson?"

Chapter 22

Willow stood inside the refrigerator box–sized polling booth, focused on the ballot. Something about blackening in the bubble next to Lauder's name filled her with happiness and heartache. How could two contradicting emotions exist inside her at the same time? Neither yielded much to the other and trying to balance them both drained her.

Her happiness was genuine and drawn from knowing how hard Lauder had worked for this, and the fact that he hadn't given up. Even when the proverbial deck was stacked against him. The heartache stemmed from seeing him in the pool the other night, laughing and enjoying life with another woman. But mainly from the notion that she'd given up on him. Given up on them.

Could she blame him for seeking comfort and support elsewhere? Her knuckles tightened around the pen she held. Yes, she could. And she did. He'd claimed to love her, too. Yet, he'd replaced her just like that. Maybe she'd handled things poorly, but so had he.

Adjusting the ball cap she'd worn to the polling station to mask her appearance, she submitted her ballot and exited the polling room. Though things had calmed, she didn't want to risk being recognized and hounded.

The first thing Willow did when she got home was kick off her shoes, grab a bag of chips and a bottle of water, curl up on the couch, and flick the television on. All the local stations were discussing the election, speculating about whether or not Lauder stood a chance. Most believed he didn't. She still held out hope.

Irritated, she changed the channel. After watching several minutes of some sappy love story that would inevitably lead to happily-ever-after like some sweet fairy tale, she growled at the screen and closed her eyes for a minute.

Willow wasn't sure how long she'd been asleep when the sound of the doorbell filtered into the dream she'd been having about Lauder. When she opened her eyes, her lips were still puckered. Why couldn't she stop thinking about him, dreaming about him, wanting him?

Collecting her thoughts, she pushed herself from the sofa. "Coming." She checked the peephole, then went still. Taking a step back, she eyed the door as if at any minute it would come flying off the hinges.

Cautiously moving back to the door, she gripped the handle, took a deep breath and pulled it open.

The first thing to greet her, after the rush of chilled air, was Lauder's delicious fragrance. Until now, she hadn't realized how much she'd missed his scent. He smelled so good goose bumps prickled her skin. The second thing to satisfy her was the way he looked in the black suit.

Ignoring her body's reaction to him, she straightened her shoulders. "Lauder?" The yielding sound of her voice irked her. Hardening her tone and firming her stance, she said, "What are you doing here?" Here, instead of at his headquarters awaiting results.

Lauder didn't utter one single word. He simply watched her intently. The longer he eyed her, the more jittery she became. Why did such an innocent observance rattle her so much?

Because there was nothing innocent about the look he gave her. It was a lot of things. Long. Hard. Penetrating. But not innocent.

"Can we talk?"

Willow parted her lips to say yes, but what came was "Who is she? The woman you were with in the pool."

"No one."

"Ah, so I imagined the two of you holding hands?"

His brow furrowed. "Is that what you thought? That we were holding hands?"

Willow arched a brow that gave an unspoken yes.

"We were giving each other a high five. We weren't together, Willow. I let you think we were because I was angry as hell with you. But I finally realized that you weren't the problem. I was. I screwed up big-time with you. I'm man enough to admit that. I should have been able to handle you needing space, but I was afraid. I'm still afraid."

"Afraid of what?"

"Of losing you. I don't want to lose you."

When Lauder's voice cracked with emotion, it triggered something tender inside her. She willed herself not to cry, but she could feel the tears welling up in her eyes. She wasn't sure she'd ever seen Lauder this vulnerable.

She wanted to wrap her arms around him, hold him tight, confess that they'd both made mistakes. "Your life would have been so much less complicated had you not run in to me that day at the coffee shop. I'm sorry."

Still stone-faced, Lauder said, "Do you regret that day?"

"The only thing I regret about that day is that it didn't happen sooner," she said without hesitation.

"Your life would be less complicated," Lauder said.

"I didn't have a life before you." Willow closed the distance between them. "Can we hug it out? Can we hug away the past two weeks?"

When Lauder wrapped his warm, strong, protective arms around her, she clung to him for dear life. The feel of him made everything right again. Her fingers clenched the fabric of his suit jacket. "God, you feel so good."

"I love you, Willow," he whispered into the crook of her neck. "I love you."

"I love you, too."

Lauder kissed her so passionately, happy tears spilled from her eyes. Her body rejoiced. Her heart rejoiced. Her soul rejoiced. She didn't want the kiss to end, but there was something she needed to say, if her words would come.

Breaking her mouth away, she cradled Lauder's face between her hands and stared into his eyes. "You deserve a woman who will always be there for you. *Especially* when times get tough." She paused. "I will be that woman, Lauder. I'll never push you away again. I love you, Lauder Tolson. More than I've ever imagined it was possible to love another human being. I. Love. You. With everything in my soul."

Lauder recaptured her mouth with a kiss so deep, so electrifying, her knees buckled. Scooping her limp body into his arms, he climbed the stairs. Anticipation swelled inside her. She wanted him so intensely she could barely think straight.

Inside the bedroom, he placed her feet on the floor. Taking his time, he undressed her, peppering kisses to random parts of her heated body. When he was done, he guided her onto the bed, then undressed himself. His dark gaze never left her as he shed piece by piece, until he stood naked in front of her. Damn, she'd missed this man. His erection suggested he'd missed her, too.

Lauder climbed onto the bed, blanketing her body with his. The feel of his warm flesh against hers aroused her even more. Her eager fingers trailed along the contours of his muscled arms. Damn, she'd really missed this man.

"I plan to satisfy every inch of your body, several times, but right now, I want, *need* to be inside of you."

"Hurry," she said, dizzy with anticipation.

When Lauder filled her, she cried out in pleasure. He delivered long, hard, fast, slow strokes. Sensations of pure ecstasy tore through her. She didn't want this moment to ever end.

"Did you miss me, baby? Did you miss me as much as I missed you?" Lauder asked, nipping the tender space below her lobe.

"Yes. Yes, Lauder, yes. So much."

"What did you miss?"

"Everything. Your scent. Your presence. Your touch. Your mouth. Your tongue. Your—"

Her words ceased when the heat of an orgasm sparked inside her, its grip growing tighter and tighter by the second. She fought it, pleaded, begged her body to hold on a little while longer. It refused, toppling her over the edge in a release so intense she couldn't breathe, couldn't see, couldn't hear.

Blood swooshed in her ears. Lauder spoke, but she couldn't make out the muffled words. Maybe he'd been trying to tell her he was coming, too, because several seconds later, he throbbed inside her. His booming grunt filtered through the swishing in her ears. Opening her eyes to see him was reminiscent of glancing up to see him standing at her table in the coffee shop. Her heart fluttered now as it had then.

Lauder leaned forward and kissed her gently on the lips, eased down next to her and pulled her still-trembling body into his arms. She closed her eyes and listened to the steady drum of his heartbeat.

"These past few weeks have been hell, Lauder. I never want to feel that kind of emptiness, loneliness again."

He glided his hand up and down her arm. "You won't. I promise. And I like keeping my promises."

A beat of silence played between them until something occurred to Willow. "Lauder, shouldn't you be at your headquarters?"

"I'm exactly where I should be."

Clearly, he'd already called the race in Edmondson's favor. Coming up on her elbow, she said, "Get dressed." She tried to roll out of bed, but he stopped her.

"Why?"

"We're going to your headquarters. It's not over until the last vote is cast. You should be there, standing shoulder to shoulder with the people who fought hard for you. Plus, Chuck is going to strangle you if you don't make an appearance."

"I'll just tell him you held me hostage."

She jostled him before inching from his hold. "Get up."

Lauder planted his feet on the floor but didn't stand. Leaning back on his elbows, he said, "For the record, I've been at my headquarters all day, but it just didn't feel right. Then I realized what the problem was."

"What was the problem?"

"You weren't there."

A smile curled Willow's lips. Their gazes held, and she could feel the potency of their connection.

"What if I told you our meeting that day in the coffee shop wasn't a coincidence?" Lauder said, sitting upright.

She slid a shirt over her head. "I would ask you to explain."

"Chuck dragged me onto social media kicking and screaming. One day, I decided to plug your name into Facebook." He shrugged. "I guess I wanted to see what your life was like. I imagined you married with several kids, a big house with a white picket fence, a dog."

Willow chuckled. "Go on."

"When your face filled the screen..." He shook his head slowly. "It was like I'd been holding my breath all of these years. Seeing you on my screen released it. You were absolutely beautiful."

She moved back to the bed and eased down beside him. Lauder took her hand into his and caressed the back with his thumb.

"There was a picture of you holding a coffee cup. The caption said, 'Hanging with my bff at our favorite coffee shop.' I recognized the Drip Drop logo on the cup."

She recalled the picture. It was one Hannah had forced her to pose for. Like Chuck had for Lauder, Hannah had dragged her kicking and screaming into the social media era, too. Boy, she was glad she had.

"I started frequenting the Drip Drop hoping to bump into you. Then one day, there you were. My world changed forever that day. A month later and after wicked macchiato addiction, here we are."

She lifted her head to look into his eyes. "Here we are."

"I have loved you so long, Willow, that I wouldn't know how to not love you if I tried."

"Don't ever try."

"I won't."

He dipped his head and kissed her. She cursed the sound of his cell phone vibrating from somewhere on the floor. Luckily, he didn't halt his delicious assault on her mouth. The vibration stopped, then started again a few seconds later.

"Your cell phone is ringing," she said against their joined mouths.

"Ignore it," he said, guiding her back down on the bed. "We're busy."

"It's probably Chuck."

Lauder groaned. "Woman, you really know how to kill a moment."

Willow laughed and pushed him up.

Fishing the phone from his pants, he answered. "What's up, Chuck? I know. Yes, I'm with her. Yes, I am."

Lauder eyed her and winked. She blew him a kiss.

"Why? Okay, okay. Baby, turn on the television, please."

The words BREAKING NEWS scrolled across the screen, followed by Edmondson being led into the police department for questioning about his involvement in Lauder's hacking scandal. His family-man charms wouldn't get him out of this one.

What was even more stunning was the fact that Lauder was in the lead by three thousand votes. Though it was still early, this was promising. Lauder still had a chance. She sent a quick prayer up for a victory.

"He withdrew?"

The words snagged Willow's attention. Had Lauder just said Edmondson withdrew? How would this affect the election?

Lauder covered the phone. "Edmondson withdrew from the race," he whispered to her. "Wait. Chuck, you didn't have anything to do with this, did you? Sorry, man. I had to ask."

Lauder stayed on the line a couple more minutes, then

ended the call. He stood silent for a moment as if trying to process everything he'd just learned.

Willow neared him but remained silent.

He ran a hand over his head. "This is crazy," he said. "I could win this thing. This is crazy," he repeated.

"So, what happens now?"

"We go to headquarters and wait."

Several hours later, Lauder's campaign headquarters erupted in cheers. Folks tossed red, white and blue confetti and blew squawkers. Balloons fell from the ceiling. All to celebrate Senator Lauder Tolson.

After giving a short speech to his team, thanking everyone for their hard work and dedication, Lauder led Willow into his office.

She yelped when he scooped her off the floor and spun her around. Burying his face in the crook of her neck, he kissed her several times. When he pulled away, a slow smile crawled across Lauder's face.

"We did it," he said.

"*You* did it. I was just along for the ride."

Lauder placed her back on her feet and held her at arm's length. "*We* did it. And I want to keep doing it with you for the rest of my life. I want you on this ride with me forever."

"I feel the same way," she said, resting her hands against his chest.

Lauder placed a hand behind her neck and pulled her close to him. "The words I'd so eloquently crafted in my head this afternoon somehow no longer seem powerful enough." He dragged a finger down the side of her face. "I have loved you since I was eight years old, Willow Dawson. My Weeping Willow."

She pinched him playfully, and he pretended to be in pain.

Sobering, he continued, "Since I was eight years old. I don't think I understood the magnitude of that until this very moment."

"Are you intentionally trying to make me cry?"

"Never in a million years would I have ever guessed I'd be here with you. Fate brought us back together. Love has bound us."

A tear slid down Willow's cheek.

"There's nothing I wouldn't do for you, Willow. Absolutely nothing."

Lauder's tone and expression were both so stern, so filled with conviction, it captured her breath.

"You make me whole, make me complete. You make me a better person, a better man. And I know you *hate* when I call you perfect, but baby, the truth is, you are perfect. So very perfect for me. In every sense of the term."

She swiped her hand across her cheek. "Well, when you put it like that..."

"Marry me, Willow."

She gasped, the words taking her completely by surprise. "What did you just say?"

"I want you to be my wife. Marry me. Please. I'll give you all that I am. I'll give you everything I have. I'll give you eternity. Marry me."

Her heart pounded in her chest. She'd heard Lauder, every word, but just couldn't believe what she was hearing. He wanted to marry her. After all they'd been through, he still wanted to marry her. Love truly was a powerful thing.

Willow rested a trembling hand on his cheek. "You're a good man, Lauder Tolson. A brave man. A strong man. A king. You have given me what no other man has ever dared to give me. Courage." Her voice cracked as she continued, "Courage to love. Love in a way I've never loved before. And I do love you. I love you in a way I've never dreamed of loving a man. In a way that doesn't seem humanly possible. My heart chose you. It will always choose you. I think we are exactly where we're meant to be, Lauder. In love with each other. And I don't want to be anywhere else. Ever. I'm lucky to have you. And nothing, *nothing* would bring me any greater joy than to call you my husband. Yes, I'll be your wife."

Lauder lifted her off her feet and spun her around again. When they stopped, he crashed his mouth against hers and kissed her as if he'd longed an eternity to touch her lips. When the kiss ended, her lips ached. She welcomed the discomfort.

Her gaze fixed on her future husband, her heart swelling with pride. "I guess we're casting one last vote tonight," she said.

"One last vote?"

"Yes. A vote for love."

Lauder scooped her into his arms again. "Baby, we've already been declared the winners. Now, we celebrate... forever."

Forever was okay with her.

Epilogue

One year later...

Willow woke to find herself alone in bed. There was only one guess as to where her husband could be. Climbing out of bed, she made her way down the hall. Tiptoeing into the nursery, she admired Lauder in silence, standing at the side of their son's crib, watching him sleep. A smile touched her lips.

Wrapping her arms around him from behind, she rested her head against his back and inhaled his scent. "I thought I would find you here."

He reached back and rested his hands on her lace-covered butt. "Hey, beautiful."

She planted several kisses on his bare back. "You okay?"

"Yeah. Yeah," he repeated. "I just wanted to check on our little man."

"You're such a doting father. And a great father. And an awesome husband."

"I couldn't do any of it without you," he said, pulling her in front of him and locking his arms around her waist. "Especially the husband part." He kissed the back of her head.

"I love you, Senator Tolson."

"I love you, Mrs. Tolson." He kissed the back of her head again. "I never imagined being a father could feel so…redeeming. I'm a father," he said as if he still couldn't believe it after all this time.

"Yes, you are, and I have the official adoption decree to prove it."

A week after the election, she and Lauder had flown to Barbados to wed. They said their "I dos" on the beach at sunset. Several months later, she'd received a call that had made her burst into tears right there on the line. An abandoned baby boy needed temporary foster placement. Days later, they'd welcomed Christopher Isaiah into their home. After unsuccessful attempts to locate any family for the child, a fast-tracked adoption had been performed. Several months after that, they'd welcomed Christopher as a permanent part of their family.

If anyone had told her her life could be this…perfect, she would have called them a liar. But it was perfect. In every sense of the term. Life was good. She'd even gotten used to being a senator's wife, and the constant invasion of privacy that came along with it.

It had been an adjustment. Reporters were constantly sniffing around in search of the next big political scandal. They wouldn't find one here.

"Let's go back to bed," Lauder said.

They each stole a kiss from their son before leaving the room.

Inside their bedroom, Willow removed a large gift-wrapped box from inside the closet and placed it next to Lauder on the bed.

"What the heck is this?" he asked.

"Your anniversary gift."

"Our anniversary isn't until Saturday."

"I can't wait that long. Open it."

"Is it an iPad Pro?" he asked.

"No."

"That wireless projector I've been dropping hints about?"

She laughed. "No."

"A printer?"

"Lauder Davenport Tolson. Just open the box."

"Okay, okay."

He tore into the wrapping and eyed the several smaller gift-wrapped boxes inside curiously, each numbered one through five.

"Start with box one," she said.

Lauder removed the wrapping from the first box and smiled. "A twenty-dollar Drip Drop gift certificate."

"Roughly a dollar for each year we were apart. And from the place where we were reunited."

"The best gift ever," he said, leaning over and pecking her gently on the lips.

"I wouldn't be so sure about that," she said. "Box two."

Immediately after seeing the contents, he flashed a sexy half smile. "Two round-trip tickets to Memphis. Okay, *this* is the best gift ever."

Willow shook her head. "Keep going."

Box three contained a heavily loaded arcade swipe card.

"You can play that claw game all night if you want," she said.

He pretended to shed a tear. "You really know the way to my heart, woman." Ripping into box four, he removed the item from inside. "A sea-shell picture frame."

"Not just any sea-shell picture frame. I had it custom-made from the shells we collected on our wedding night beach walk in Barbados."

Lauder ran a finger over the piece. "Okay, I was wrong. Hands down, *this* is the best gift ever."

Willow didn't challenge him this time. Though, she had an idea that he would have a change of heart after opening box five.

"Box five," he said. "The only thing that could top the picture frame is keys to that Bugatti you won't let me buy." He shook the box. "Doesn't sound like keys. Drumroll, please." He cleared his throat. "Drumroll, woman."

"Oh. You're serious?"

"Uh, yeah."

She laughed. "You are so dramatic." Making some awful sound with her mouth—and feeling quite ridiculous for entertaining Lauder's silly request—she watched him tear into the last gift.

Lauder's jaw went slack, his eyes slowly rising to meet hers. "Is this…" He massaged the back of his neck with his hand. "Are you—" His voice cracked. "You're pregnant?"

She nodded, her eyes clouding with tears. "Our family is growing. I recall you once saying something about wanting an army."

Pushing the gift debris aside, Lauder pulled her into his arms and hugged her so tight she thought she would melt into his chest. He buried his face in the crook of her neck. A second later, she felt his warm tears on her shoulder.

"I love you, Willow. I will love you until my very last breath."

She knew that he would.

* * * * *

COMING SOON!

We really hope you enjoyed reading this book. If you're looking for more romance, be sure to head to the shops when new books are available on

Thursday
23rd August

To see which titles are coming soon, please visit
millsandboon.co.uk

MILLS & BOON

Coming next month

THE MILLION POUND MARRIAGE DEAL
Michelle Douglas

Sophie had had good sex before, but what she shared with Will wasn't just good. It was *spectacular*. She hadn't known it could be like this.

Not that she said that to Will, of course. It smacked too much of a neediness that would send him running for the hills. She didn't want him running for the hills. Not yet.

Not that they spent all their time in bed. They spent hours riding Magnus and Annabelle as he showed her all the places he'd loved when he was young. They explored the glens and the hills, traversed lochs and cantered through crystal-clear streams. They spent hours playing board games and watching musicals with Carol Ann.

But when they retired to their room each night — they made love as if they never wanted to stop. Not just once, but again and again. As if they couldn't get enough of each other. As if they were addicted.

It wasn't until Thursday, though, that Sophie finally realised how much trouble she was in. When Will told her he had to go back to London the next day. The depth of the protest that rose through her had her clutching the wedding folder she held to her chest. As casually as she could, she leant a shoulder against the bedroom doorframe to counter the sensation of falling, of dizziness. Loss, anguish and despair all pounded through her.

Will sat on the side of the bed, his back to her, pulling on his shoes, so she allowed herself precisely three seconds to close her eyes and drag in a breath, to pull herself together. 'No rest for the wicked?' she forced herself to ask, with award-winning composure.

He didn't move and she tried to paste what she hoped was a cheeky grin into place. 'I suppose I should be focusing on the wedding anyway. Nine days, Will. The month has flown!'

He turned, a frown in his eyes. 'Do you want to back out?'

'Of course not.' It was just... She hadn't known when she'd agreed to this paper marriage that she'd be marrying the man she *loved*. 'Do you?'

Continue reading
THE MILLION POUND MARRIAGE DEAL
Michelle Douglas

Available next month
www.millsandboon.co.uk

LET'S TALK
Romance

For exclusive extracts, competitions
and special offers, find us online:

  facebook.com/millsandboon

@millsandboonuk

@millsandboon

Or get in touch on 0844 844 1351*

For all the latest titles coming soon, visit
millsandboon.co.uk/nextmonth